
PLAYING FOR KEEPS

JUNO CHASE

E-book ISBN 978-1-947234-00-0

Print ISBN: 978-1-947234-19-2

I feel like a part of my soul has loved you since the beginning of everything. Maybe we're from the same star.

–Emery Allen

Chapter 1

Katherine loved being out with the girls for a night out on the town. She had worked hard the last week in DC --- she was the senior legislative assistant for Congressman Lincoln Ulysses Pierce---and now she was ready to blow off some steam. She had come to New York City to visit her sorority sisters for their usual monthly girl's weekend. Their favorite starter bar, Nico's, was crowded. It was a classy and quiet joint in comparison with the clubs they would go to later. The music was just loud enough to keep their conversations from being overheard in the booths nearby, and quiet enough they didn't have to yell at each other to be heard.

Their favorite waitress usually kept a table for them. They'd been later than usual, though, so they'd had to wait at the bar for a table to open up. She led them to a booth, and Katherine sank into the plush velvet seat. Her two closest sorority sisters, Vanessa and Ashley flanked her on each side. They'd ordered their drinks at the bar and moved as their booth had become available. Nico's was the perfect place where she and her sorority sisters could get caught up on their lives before hitting the dance scene. Not only could they talk, but the appetizers were delicious.

Vanessa scooted in close so she could be heard. She laid her hand on the table, and her diamond bracelet flashed in the light. Vanessa had been born with a silver spoon, and with Kat, she had always been the most loyal, and direct. "I'm still not clear on this game thing. Why wouldn't the person who is best qualified to go on the trip be asked to go?"

One of her co-workers, Madeline, had suggested that they play a BINGO game to determine who would go to a top-secret meeting in Vegas. This kind of deal would be a boon for her career. She would get the chance to meet with two billionaire entrepreneurs who were interested in changing the way American industry transports goods.

Normally, they would never have the women in their office play a BINGO game to decide who would go to something like this, but this game seemed pretty harmless. She wanted the playing field to be even — well she wanted the playing field to be in her favor, and she knew she could easily win. In this case, the game she and her office mates were playing was straight-forward. To win BINGO, Kat had to kiss five different guys at five different monuments. The winner of BINGO went with Congressman Pierce to Vegas. After working there for eight years, Katherine knew everyone in D.C., the game should be easy to win.

"Link, or Congressman Pierce, gives the office staff some autonomy in how certain projects play out. Of course, he doesn't know we are playing BINGO. He probably thinks we're running through a list of all our qualifications."

"Honestly, Katherine, I can see why you're drinking hard liquor," Ashley said with a southern drawl thickened by wine. "Those people you work with don't seem to be straight shooters. I would probably tear my hair out if I had to deal with all these games you keep telling us about. Why couldn't you do something easier, like draw straws?"

"I want to know how it's done, though," Vanessa said. "I mean, did you actually print out BINGO cards for this? I'm confused."

Katherine rummaged through her purse and found

her Bingo card. "See? We came up with all kinds of jobs people do in D.C. to replace the numbers on the cards, and five monuments for the BINGO letters." She drew her finger along the top and tapped at the individual squares for emphasis. She had crossed out three squares across the diagonal.

They were all decent enough men who were all easily and completely 'friend-zoned' by the end their short dates. "We have to take a man with the occupation underneath each of the monuments across the top for a kiss. Whoever fills out a BINGO first gets to go to this top-secret meeting."

"You have to go out on five dates and manage to get these five guys to go to five different monuments and kiss you?" Vanessa asked.

Katherine wasn't sure she could make it any clearer, but she tried anyway. "It's one guy per monument. Unless I can't fill up a row and need to start with a different row. I might have to take the second date to a monument I've been to in order to get a different row."

"Oh, hey, you didn't leave the free space in the middle," Ashley said. "That makes it harder."

Katherine looked at her for a long moment. "I don't know what you're talking about."

"The free space in the middle." Ashley rolled her eyes and sighed in exasperation. "Kat, regular BINGO cards leave the middle square as a freebie to help people along. You'd have four out of five if you had the freebie."

Katherine wouldn't know about that. She hadn't actually played a game of Bingo since she was in elementary school. "You seem to know an awful lot about BINGO, Ashley."

"I told you Carville is a small place. BINGO is a big deal there. I might have played a time or two."

"Are you hanging out at the retirement homes now for fun?" she asked, teasing Ashley. Images of old people with cards spread out in front of them, giant markers in hand ready to stamp flashed through Katherine's head. She'd seen it on television plenty of times. Bingo was usually for old people. The game she was playing was decidedly not regular Bingo. "Ashley, please tell me you are not turning into a Bingo Parlor Queen."

Ashley pointed to Kat's Bingo card. "Look who's talking about being a Bingo Queen?"

Kat laughed easily. "Okay okay, you have a point."

Vanessa grabbed the card from Katherine and turned it toward the light behind them. She would never admit to needing glasses. "Okay, so from this it looks like you've been out with a reporter, a guy from homeland security, and a lawyer. *All in the last week?*

You have been having some fun. So jealous. I'd totally love playing this game."

Katherine held up her martini in a toasting gesture before knocking back the rest of the contents.

Ashley raised her perfectly shaped eyebrows and blinked rapidly for emphasis. "Thirsty dear?"

If they only knew what it had cost her to join them in New York for their regular girly weekend out. "That's right. Three dates in a week. One of them was just lunch. Two were on the same day." Plus, working until midnight every night just so she would be free for this weekend.

Ashley reached for the card and examined it again. "You work with lobbyists all the time, don't you? I would think that would have been your first mark on the card."

"Oh, there are plenty of lobbyists in the world, but most of them are sleaze-buckets. I've been dreading picking one. One of them totally came on to our newest intern this week, tried to lure her away with the promise of big bucks after graduation and everything— got into a brawl with one of my favorite attorneys. Fuckwad."

"The attorney or the lobbyist?" Vanessa asked.

"Ha. The lobbyist. Total asshat. The attorney? He's a sweetheart. Seriously. He's like the only one in DC that I really adore. He's out to save the world through good deeds. But yeah, the lobbyist involved is a total piece of work."

"And, this CIA guy, do you have to get a spy or can anyone from the agency make do?" Ashley asked.

Katherine took the card from Ashley and shoved it back in her purse. Why had she even brought it with her? It's not like she was going to be able to make any progress while in New York. She had it memorized and didn't need to look at it any more. "Anyone from the CIA will do. The only people who admit they work for the CIA are tech and admin support people, and maybe retired spooks. Field agents aren't walking around with big signs on their foreheads."

"I know that, silly. But it would be exciting to date a spy, wouldn't it?" Ashley asked. "A real life James Bond."

There was something wistful about the look in her eyes that put Katherine on edge. Ashley had gotten into some dangerous relationships with 'bad boys' in the past. "Please don't get any ideas about looking for one." Kat swept a stray hair behind Ashley's ear. She would get eaten alive in D.C.

"I can't believe you would all go to such an effort for a stupid meeting. It's kind of ridiculous, don't you think?" Vanessa asked.

"It made perfect sense when we started it," Katherine said. And it had, too. As the senior legislative assistant in Congressman Lincoln Pierce's office, Katherine spent most of her days holed up in her office reading draft legislation.

Until recently, her primary job had been making sure the Congressman understood every bill that he would be voting on. Even though he was, himself, an attorney, he didn't have time to do the heavy research required. The last week, however, she'd been pulled in to help with the final stages of a bill the congressman was trying to push through. The final step involved a set of hearings that would address various environmental impacts of the bill. The hearings had been moved up two weeks, and she'd almost missed this trip to New York because of all the extra work. She'd have to haul ass to get everything ready by Wednesday morning.

"What's this meeting in Vegas about, anyway?" Vanessa asked.

"It's a top-secret meeting. I can't give you any details."

"If it's so top secret, why are you even telling us about the game?" Ashley asked.

"It's not like I'm giving you any details, but maybe I shouldn't have said anything. You all need to keep it to yourselves, Okay? Let's talk about something else, shall we? Like, why is it just the three of us tonight? I thought everyone was coming this weekend."

Vanessa flopped back and ran her hands through her hair. "Well, the others are straggling in. I bet Sarah is asleep at the loft already. Lacy and Willow are coming early tomorrow morning. There's no way those two would miss brunch or the spa."

Chapter 2

The waitress cleared away their glasses, wiped down the table, and took their new orders. A guy at the table next to them pinched her bottom, and Kat about jumped out of her seat to go slap him, but the other two penned her in. The waitress skittered out of reach with a smile on her face.

"Did you see that?" Katherine hissed at the other two.

"Yeah. Real creeper. He's drunk, Kat. Don't get involved. Besides, Molly can handle herself." Ashley sighed, then visibly cheered as she changed the subject. "Lacy swears she'll keep coming after the wedding. Dex was there, and he said that he didn't own her, and she could do whatever she wanted. I think he's one of the good ones."

The group had been flying to New York every month since they'd graduated from college. Vanessa had a huge penthouse apartment in one of her father's buildings she called 'The Loft' even though it was a ten-thousand square foot, two-floor house inside a building in New York City, not really an apartment at all. Certainly not a loft in the traditional sense.

Vanessa usually occupied a tenth of the apartment, and opened the whole thing up each month to her sorority sisters. One by one, their number had dropped from twelve down to six regulars--Katherine, Vanessa, Ashley, Sarah, Lacy, and Willow. There'd been six weddings and ten babies from the group over the last six years, and the married women inevitably stopped coming to their weekend parties.

Usually they came until they had a baby before dropping out in spite of their husbands not liking them having a wild weekend with the girls. Mostly, the new moms were too tired from raising kids to truly enjoy the partying and just wanted to relax instead.

Katherine could understand that particular kind of tired, having experienced it as the oldest of ten kids. Helping her mom with the younger children had given Katherine her fill of babies and was the main reason she didn't want to have any of her own. Ever.

A corner of Kat's closet was stuffed silly with

unusable bridesmaid's dresses as souvenirs. Katherine would never willingly buy any of the dresses she'd bought for her sorority sisters' weddings. She certainly wouldn't wear any of them more than once, not even to the several soirees held around D.C. She held onto them solely for the memories--and maybe for Halloween costumes.

Katherine looked forward to picking out a hideous bridesmaid dress to burden their closets with. Maybe something with flower roses or bows, harkening back to the eighties just for fun. It had turned into a competition between them—who would find the ugliest shade of mauve? Who would find the most outrageous bow to plaster across their bottoms? Who would find the puffiest sleeves?

She hated to admit it to herself--she wanted to believe that all she wanted was a fantastic career--but she wanted the man and the wedding. She wanted the man of her dreams, even if she didn't know what that meant exactly. Her dreams had never defined him for her. She knew he would be good looking, smart, and capable of living with her career—capable of being an equal partner to a woman who was rising to the top. And, of course, he had to be someone who was cool without having kids. The chances of meeting someone like that wasn't going to happen, but she was not about to alter her standards either.

She wanted the *Big Wedding*, with all twelve of the original Tri-Delts in ridiculous dresses at her side. She wanted a multi-layered cake with six different flavors that towered over the room. She wanted ten different buffet tables piled with foods from all around the world. She wanted dancing until the wee hours of the morning, where she and her groom took to the floor like a Patrick Swayze movie.

Nobody puts Kat in a corner.

And the honeymoon. She wanted a honeymoon somewhere warm with sandy beaches, sapphire blue and emerald water, and jewel-toned tropical fish. And she wanted to drink alcohol out of a coconut with a straw and suck pineapple chunks off an umbrella toothpick.

Whenever she imagined any of this, the man's head was fuzzed out. Blurry and undefined. Who would he be?

"Kitty-Kat?"

She only let a small handful of people call her Kitty-Kat. Two of them were sitting next to her. "I'm sorry. Missed that."

"I was asking about Marshall? How's he doing? Have you told him about this kissing game thing?" Ashley asked, eyes wide. "Doesn't he care you're going out on all these dates with other men?"

Katherine swirled the toothpick holding a thin

slice of cucumber in the newest drink the waitress had just brought. She needed to come clean with these guys. "You know...I have something to tell you about Marshall."

Vanessa slapped her hand flat on the table. "I knew it. I. Knew. It. Seriously. You made him up. Didn't you?"

Vanessa was her closest friend. If anyone was going to figure it out, it would be her.

Katherine hung her head. She wasn't about to tell her sorority girls that she was on six different dating sites and had gone out with a long string of men who all wanted to father her children. She wasn't about to tell them how she'd learned to delete any guy who had interest in kids or had children already. She had finally changed her profile to be as clear as possible. It reduced the dating pool a lot when you put 'you must have a vasectomy to date me' front and center on your profile page.

Instead of admitting her massive dating failures to her friends, she had made up someone named Marshall. Each month she gave them tidbits about a guy she'd cobbled together from the best parts of the men she had found mostly lacking. She wasn't sure if such a man could exist in the real world.

"I was tired of having nothing to talk about every time we got together."

Vanessa pumped her fist in the air. "I knew he was too perfect sounding. It was like you plucked him out of some stupid romance novel."

Ashley grabbed Katherine's hand and gave Vanessa the stinky eye. Ashley simply couldn't pull off mean with any veracity—she was the very essence of sweet if not wholly innocent. "But why? You know we'll love you anyway. Whether you have a beau or not."

Ashley's adorable southern accent had doubled once she'd moved back home. She was a Georgian girl through and through. She seemed to have it all. She was a director of sales at a famous whiskey maker, even though she technically lived in a dry county--a dry county in the middle of absolutely no-where-ville with mostly older married men. Men her age had fled to bigger cities and opportunity.

In spite of all that, Ashley had a steady boyfriend. Okay, man friend. What did you call a man you were dating when he was forty-nine and you were just barely thirty, anyway? Katherine couldn't do it, but there were definite perks to being steady with a man who was done growing up.

"I just didn't want your pity anymore. Everyone is either getting married or engaged or otherwise paired off. You were beginning to feel sorry for me. Calling me an old maid, even nicely, doesn't help, Ashley."

"I'm not paired off," Vanessa said. "And I'm happy being single. A new guy every couple of months..." Her voice trailed off as she eyed a group of men leaving the bar. "How did we miss *them*? Meow."

Ashley tsked and focused her attention on Katherine. "Are you still doing that thing you do? You know...the no *real-sex* thing?"

Warmth flooded Katherine's cheeks. It sounded weirder when Ashley said it aloud like that. "I have sex. I just don't let them stick their dicks inside me."

She gave Vanessa a side look that warned her to be quiet. Vanessa was the only one who knew the real reason why she was so paranoid about it all. Pregnancy. She was deathly afraid of it. Not *pregnancy* itself but the child that would pop out at the end. In college, she took the pill faithfully thinking it would be enough. And it was, right up until the one time when she was a few days late with her period—something that never happened. She peed on a stick, and two bright blue lines appeared almost immediately—the test showed positive.

She wallowed in the terror of being pregnant for a couple of weeks before going to a doctor. She was miserable, physically and mentally, but it turned out to have been a false alarm. A blood test proved she wasn't actually pregnant. Her period didn't come for another month after that, but Katherine had already decided she'd never let a man inside her again unless he had written proof of a vasectomy.

Vanessa winked at her. "I was actually beginning to think you were boinking that hot Congressman you work for and were covering with this Marshall business."

Katherine dropped her jaw open. "Oh. God. No. I mean, yeah he's hot, but he's totally off-limits."

"Is he? Does he have someone?" Ashley asked.

"No, no one steady, but he's got a really strict policy that no one can go near him. No one in the office, anyway. He dates. And he dates really gorgeous women."

"I've seen photos of them. None of them are as pretty as you are, Katherine," Vanessa said.

Katherine closed her eyes. "No. No. No. You guys don't get it. I want to keep working for him. I think he's going to be president someday, and I'd much rather be working for him than sleeping with him."

"President? So, you'd be, like, chief of staff or something? Like that Cyrus Bean character on Scandal?" Ashley's eyes were round with excitement.

"Exactly. Except without all that craziness involving killing people. For crying out loud, television is all made up, you do know that right?"

Ashley shrank back a little, shaking her head. "I don't think it's as made up as you think it is."

"Sure, some back-room deals are made, but nothing really like in the show. They are just a bunch of writers making up the worst possible scenarios that could happen in politics. Come on Ashley, you don't believe that stuff, do you?" Katherine wasn't quite sure just how conspiracy theory minded Ashley was these days. It was hard to tell when you only saw someone once a month. "Look, Link, I mean, Congressman Pierce, is a good man. He will be the next best president to come our way. He's ethical, honest, and truly wanting to see the best things for this country."

"Sounds like you are crushing on him, Kitty-Kat." Vanessa tossed back the last of her wine, caught the eye of the waitress and pointed at her empty glass.

"You would if you knew him. But, as you know, I'm quite fine without real man-flesh between my legs. I get plenty of satisfaction with men as it is. I don't need them inside me."

"Sweetie, you keep saying that, and you might even have convinced yourself you don't miss it," said Vanessa. "Maybe, it's just that you've gone so long without the real thing, you're fooling yourself."

"Yeah," added Ashley, a breathy wistfulness to her voice. "There's nothing like a sweaty man to grab onto while you know, he's doing his thing. Besides, I think if you were really into a guy, you'd be begging him to fuck you. You just haven't found him. So darlin', what you need is to find *that guy*."

Chapter 3

*V*anessa stood up. "Who's watching the table? I need to go to the bathroom."

Katherine waved her hand, dismissing them both. "Don't worry, I'll guard your booze."

Kat tried her best to hide her annoyance. They just didn't get it.

Neither of them seemed to understand that she could have plenty of mind-blowing orgasms. Sexy times with men didn't always have to include intercourse. Anyone who thought penis in vagina was the pinnacle of sex must have a pretty boring sex life. The notion that she would ever limit herself just to that again made her laugh. Once she'd sworn off allowing men inside her, she had to get creative out of necessity to keep the men in her life happy--as well as herself. Very few had complained. She felt sorry for

Ashley and Vanessa. They were the ones missing out, not her.

She drained her martini as they made their way to the bathroom. She looked around for the waitress, but couldn't find her. Kat checked her texts and her email, relieved there was no new emergency at the office. Just as she was finishing, a man approached her table and carefully set a fresh martini in front of her.

Now this was unusual. Most guys would send the server over and wait for the nod before coming over. This guy had brought his gift himself.

"Bartender said you were drinking these tonight. I'm not convinced cucumber ever belongs in a glass, but who I am to argue with a beautiful woman?"

Katherine counted to five before looking up, expecting to engage with a self-satisfied smugness. Instead, she was engulfed by vibrant green eyes dancing with humor.

The world slowed and dimmed to a quiet darkness on the periphery of her vision. The bar muted. The clinking of glasses, the buzz of voices, the unobtrusive music, all of it dialed down to a muffled indistinct undertone. She could only hear the beating of her heart, thumping. Thumping. Thumping.

That *thing* she'd read about in books, that *thing* that people have talked about but she had never experienced, that *thing* that she'd always dreamed about, that she craved-- that *thing* filled the space between them. It was an invisible current binding them, holding them, connecting them.

Even as it happened, she recognized it. There was something communicated between them, though she wasn't entirely sure what it was. The closest she could come to describe it was a profound knowing.

And it freaked her out. She wanted to jump up and run away. She also wanted to sink into the tangled forest of his eyes and stay there forever.

A shrill laugh from the corner of the room woke her from the augmented state of reality.

"Thank you," she said, finally. Was it minutes or seconds since he'd set the drink down?

He straightened his tie and cleared his throat. A thick dark curl tumbled across his bronzed forehead as he nodded at her. "You're welcome. I expect your posse is coming back soon. Perhaps we could meet up for a dance somewhere later on."

She was nodding as he spoke, a numb trance-like euphoria had settled over her, keeping her in her seat. She wanted to savor the moment as much as she wanted to flee from it.

Speaking was impossible. She took a sip of the martini he brought her. The cool, sharp liquid worked out the knot in her throat. "I think I'd like that." Her voice was smooth and warm from the liquor. "I'm

Katherine." She sounded surprised to herself, surprised and stunned.

She wanted to run a finger along his jaw, just to see if it would cut her. Katherine had a fondness for men with a strong jaw and full lips. Such kissable lips. She took another sip of the martini, trying to quell the images flooding her mind and heating up her body. If they were in D.C. she'd be dragging him to all five of the monuments in the game—he was probably some profession that was on the Bingo card. She wanted to feel the stubble on his cheek against her neck.

He held out his hand. "I'm Jerry."

She put her hand in his, a spark of tingling energy shot up her arm and warmed her whole body. "Jerry?" she repeated, dumbfounded. This broad-shouldered, chiseled man should be named Apollo, or Phoenix or Zeus--not *Jerry*. The physical connection was at odds with the images of other Jerry's she'd known popping into her head. His name was just so...wrong. She chastised her shallowness. What's in a name? Everything else about him was perfection.

His smile tightened as he winced a little. "*Close enough*. Sooooo...Katherine. Local or visiting?" He covered her hand with his other and squeezed before letting her go.

"I'm up from D.C. for the weekend."

"Small world. I'm actually moving there for work soon."

"Oh dear. Poor you."

"Poor me? Why would you say that?"

Katherine regretted the comment as soon as it was out of her mouth. The martinis had loosened her tongue. It wasn't like her to speak first and think second. "Well, you go to D.C. to do some good, to make changes in the world, you know? But then you get there and you find out it's really about the money. It's gotten so the damn lobbyists and lawyers control everything. It's exhausting trying to find people who are real. You know?"

He tilted his head toward her, eyes narrowing so that the green faded into an inky black. She'd gone overboard. Something she'd said had hit a nerve with him. She raked her eyes up and down him, getting a second measure of him. Suit and tie were custom fit and high quality. Ninety-percent likely he was a lawyer or a lobbyist. Damn.

Katherine sighed, wondering how she could pull her foot out of her over-stuffed mouth. "Sorry. I don't mean to offend. It's been a rough week for me, and I really can get on a rant at times. Ignore all that. There are actually plenty of people working to do good in D.C. What do you do? Please don't be a lawyer..."

He slid into the booth next to her, but stayed

balanced near the edge rather than settling in completely. "Actually, I'm a scientist. I work for a company in New Jersey. I'm out with my brother and a buddy celebrating my brother's recent graduation and new job."

Katherine felt a little flutter of excitement and relief. She'd just dissed lobbyists and lawyers, and maybe everyone else in D.C., but not scientists. Smart men were a major turn on for her. Oh, and what a smile. Everything about this guy was hitting her shiver-buttons.

Kat took another sip of her martini, and ran her tongue along her teeth hoping she'd caught all the poppy seeds from her lemon and poppy seed muffin she'd called dinner on the plane. She tilted her head to the bar where his two friends were watching them with the same intensity they might a boxing match. She'd seen this general scenario before. "So, Mr. Scientist, did you come over here as some part of a bar bet?"

His left lip quirked upward, rendering him utterly adorable.

"They bet I couldn't get your number."

"Right."

"No. Seriously. We were all betting that you're here for a bachelorette party for pre-marital shenanigans. The one on the left? That's Carl, my little brother. He was certain you're the bride to be."

Carl was about the same height as his brother but that's where the similarities ended. Jerry's dark, barely tamed locks contrasted with his brother's blond buzz cut. Carl's blue eyes were as bright as the sky on a clear day.

"Don't they know anything? Girls never leave the bride-to-be alone to guard the table."

"That's what I told them."

The men were lounging with their backs against the bar, leaning on their elbows, gaping at them openly.

She held out her hand. "Give me your phone."

"You don't have to. But, I'll definitely take it." As he swiped his phone awake, an image of Neil deGrasse Tyson popped up as his front screen. She held his wrist and looked at it before he could thumb in his passcode.

"Seriously? You have Neil deGrasse Tyson as your screen saver?"

"You have no idea how sexy it is that you know his name."

Their eyes met again. A flicker of that sensation that had engulfed her earlier flared between them. Maybe she looked calm and cool to him, but her center was hot, burning hot.

"He's a personal hero of mine. One of the reasons I went into science."

"He's amazing," she said as she typed in her number and sent a text to herself. The message chime tinkled from her purse.

"Katherine," he asked, waiting for her to look up from the phone and into his eyes, "do you believe in love at first sight?"

Normally, she would consider that a corny line, but he said it with such honesty, it unnerved her. Her heart stopped for about five seconds, she was sure of it.

"Is that what this is?" She wiggled her fingers in the space between the two of them.

"I don't know. Maybe." His eyes were fixed on her, unwavering. Penetrating.

"You feel it, too, don't you?" The startled fear that had threatened to overtake her earlier put her into sudden protective mode. *Make him say it first. He's the one who brought up love at first sight.*

"Feel what, exactly?" he asked. His expression so intent that she could have sworn there was no one else in the bar. It felt as if they were the only two people in the room. In the world. How could she describe the tightness in her chest? The warmth flooding her body? The pulsing buzzing in her head?

Vanessa and Ashley emerged from the bathroom, their laughter startling Kat out of the moment.

"We're heading over to Provoc next," she told Jerry.

"Save me a dance." He was already back at the bar

with his friends before the girls reached the table. He was a gentleman. His friends tried to high-five him, but he wouldn't engage and shrugged them off. Even as he tried to be serious with his friends, that smile of his told her everything she needed to know.

"Holy shit, Kat. Who is that?" Vanessa asked.

"Just some guy...."

"You looked pretty cozy with him," Ashley said.

"We were geeking out over Neil deGrasse Tyson."

"As in the Boxer?" asked Vanessa.

Ashley laughed. "No, no honey, weren't you listening? The boxer is Mike. Kat said *Neil deGrasse* Tyson, the super hunky science-space guy, you know, the new Carl Sagan."

"Whatever," Vanessa said. "Even if he's a geek, he's adorable."

Adorable was not the word Katherine would apply to Jerry. She rolled the name around in her head. She didn't really have to get used to it, or use it much. It wasn't like she was going to marry the guy.

"I hope you told him where we're heading. He and his friends might be a geek-squad, but they certainly don't look geeky."

She snuck a peek at the guys at the bar. Kat wondered why the trio didn't just come over to their table.

She looked at her friends objectively for a moment.

Yeah, there was no way she'd want to approach all three of them either. They were dressed for a smoking night out on the town. Or, as her mom would say "dressed to the nines." Katherine had looked the phrase up once, but still didn't understand what nines and perfection had to do with each other.

They all wore designer couture that outlined their figures, dresses that accentuated their asses, curved tightly against their waistlines--and the cleavage at this table? Holy shit. As a whole, they presented in a way that could definitely be intimidating. Desperate was not a word that could be used to describe any of them, even on their worst night.

They'd all dressed for clubbing. From the front, Kat's dress looked almost demure, but the back was completely bare with a sharp V as far down as it could go and still be decent. When she danced though, she wasn't entirely sure that it was all covered up, nor did she care. The slit up the right side of the dress was up to the top of her thigh high stockings, but those were only visible if she chose them to be. She wore a single diamond pendant that hung between her breasts, high-lighting the fact that she had them without actually showing them.

Vanessa, on the other hand, was wearing an almost reverse version of her dress. Her neckline plunged so low that the only thing that kept it from popping off was a metal clip just below her breasts. Without it, her dress would have gaped open as a show all. It had the same effect on men, and most took their time checking her out as they walked by.

Ashley chose a banded stripe thing that fit her like a second skin. If Kat swung toward women, she'd definitely have a crush on Ashley. She was, by far, the prettiest of the girls in the group.

Kat always felt a little like the poor step-kid of the group. She was the only one that didn't have oodles of money lying around. Her dress was from a website specializing in knock-offs of high-end designers, while her friends wore the originals. They didn't know, and she didn't think they would care. But it kind of mattered to her.

They finished their drinks and headed out to their limo. Jerry smiled at her as she passed him. He gave her a slight, almost imperceptible nod. The look in his eyes was a promise that terrified and excited her. She knew he was coming for her.

Chapter 4

The girls had dispersed onto the dance floor at Provoc, and Katherine was dancing with a short German guy who barely spoke English. Jerry and his buddies showed up halfway through the song, but she was the kind of girl that saw things through. She finished her half-dance half-charade with the German guy as politely as she could. She caught Ashley and Vanessa's attention and nodded toward the guys.

The three women converged at the bar and introductions were made all around. It was much easier to pair off with equal numbers, even though the other two men looked a little dumbfounded at having been approached by the trio of gorgeous women.

"We're actually about to leave, so, if you want that

dance, you better get it now." She wanted to see if he could handle her.

Jerry held out his hand in a classic invitation to dance gesture, palm up. "You know I do."

Warmth radiated up her arm and pulsed through her body. She had never had this kind of reaction before, where she wanted to melt at the barest of touches. The group headed to the dance floor, a trio of pairs circling around each other as they grooved to the music.

"Thanks for bringing Ashley and Vanessa over. Carl and Glen are like middle-school boys who are too shy to ask a girl to dance."

"Yeah, we actually tend to like wall-flowers."

The music shifted into something slow, and Jerry reached for her, settling them into a formal fox-trot position. She was impressed. Most men defaulted to the high school version of slow-dancing with their arms draped around each other's necks and swaying from foot to foot.

Jerry's fingers pressed into her back, warm and hot, but soft and comforting at the same time. Her body reacted almost immediately, and she couldn't believe the wetness between her legs. She relaxed into his arms and let him lead her.

"You've taken dance lessons," she said.

"My mother made me. She was old-fashioned."

"You know how to rhumba and cha-cha?" she asked, lifting her heel and baring her leg through the sky-high slit.

"I do," he said, trying to hide his smile.

"How would it go over if we slipped out of here and went over to a salsa club?"

The music wasn't a rhumba, but he shifted into flawless Cuban motion anyway. Within a couple of beats, she was taking his lead, their hips swaying together in the sexiest dance movements on the planet. He slid his hands to her hips to an alternate position, taking them from the formal boxier form to something much more intimate.

"Let's get out of here," he said.

"I need to let the girls know where I'm going."

"Salsa?" Vanessa asked. She cast an appraising glance at Carl. "Sounds like fun. We're all going, though. Carl? Glen? You ready to dance all night?"

They gathered everyone and stumbled out of the massively popular club into the cool air. Vanessa's limo appeared around the corner. Carl whistled as the driver opened the door and ushered them all into the car.

"Being Vanessa's friend definitely has its perks," said Ashley.

"You mean this isn't a rental for the evening?" Carl asked.

"Oh, honey. Bless your heart, Carl. Aren't you the sweetest thing ever?" She pinched his cheek.

Jerry ushered Ashley and Katherine into their row before settling himself in next to Katherine.

Vanessa was sandwiched between Carl and Glen. She was obviously excited to be between the two men. Vanessa was more than a little experienced handling two guys at the same time--literally. She'd shared the details of her ménages plenty of time with the group. Katherine shook her head and rolled her eyes at Vanessa. Kat had no problem with *other* people doing the threesome thing, but she wasn't into it personally.

"Tell me, Carl, what do you do for a living?" asked Vanessa. Katherine could tell she was interested.

Carl touched his nose in a motion that told Katherine he was used to pushing glasses upward as a way to cover his obvious nervousness. The only thing was, he wasn't wearing any glasses.

Vanessa chuckled. "Carl, you just graduated, right? Where from? How old are you?"

Carl blinked at the onslaught of questions. "I'm twenty-two."

Jerry patted Carl on the knee. "He graduated last weekend from Brandeis and started this week at his first real job. No break in between. Glen and I brought him out to celebrate. He's green in a lot of ways."

Vanessa moved in on him like a snake on a pinkie.

"Well, I'm happy to help make this a memorable weekend."

She squeezed his knee.

Carl's cheeks turned a deep shade of red, but he smiled brightly. While Carl might be green, he certainly had enough confidence.

Katherine shifted until she was leaning against Jerry. She breathed in his scent. A few hours past fresh, but whatever cologne or aftershave he was wearing was musky in a way that she liked. The slight sweat he'd worked up on the dance floor had a manly earthiness to it that turned her on.

"You ready for more dancing?" he asked.

"Yes. I haven't had a good rhumba in a very long time." The way she said good rhumba could be taken entirely the wrong way, and she blushed a little at the double entendre.

He laughed, and she felt the rumble against her cheek as she leaned against his chest. It was rich and grounding. She imagined what he would sound like, groaning in pleasure, how his voice would feel through her hands and what his mouth would taste like. She looked up at him, expecting that he might kiss her, wanting him to. But, he didn't. Instead, he traced her lips with his index finger. A light, gentle touch that tickled and kindled a keen, pulsing, desire.

The limo arrived at the Latin club where the

neon sign proclaimed the music would be all Latin all the time-- salsa, cha-cha, rhumba, and tango. They'd probably play the Macarena every now and again, an oldie but a goodie to get the crowd revved up.

It was getting very late, or really early, depending on how you count your time, and the crowd was dwindling, so they had no problem finding a large table in a corner. The others settled into the table to order drinks. Jerry held out his hand to Katherine before she had a chance to sit down. He spun her away from the group and toward the dance floor like a pro. His frame was perfectly formal, yet every motion sent tingles of anticipation through her body.

He led her through every dance move she had ever learned and quite a few combinations she'd never seen. For once, she was glad that her mother insisted she take lessons from an early age. Jerry was as good as anyone she'd ever danced with before.

Jerry was in total control. His frame was perfect, and even when she tried to take the lead, she couldn't. He wouldn't let her.

Even after three rhumbas and two electrifying cha-chas, she wasn't wanting or needing a break. They were in a groove, and they were getting attention from others. People stopped dancing to watch them glide and swoop across the floor, just like in the movies. She had never danced with anyone who made her look this amazing, this graceful.

She had never danced with anyone who made her feel so complete. He was even better than the guy she imagined she'd dance with at her wedding.

Finally, the music shifted into a Tango. Jerry paused and pulled her in close, placing his forehead against hers. His body spoke to her through his fingers, his arms, his hips. Her body knew exactly how to respond. It was like they were two halves of a whole, she fit him perfectly.

The real world around them took on a mystical, ethereal quality. The only thing in focus was Jerry. The music guided them, but she hardly heard the melody. It was subsumed by the passion of the connection between them.

They improvised, her dancing away from him, him spinning her back effortlessly. She wrapped her leg around his waist, and he dipped her backward until her hair brushed the floor. His erection pressed against her as he held her close. His green eyes intensified, and she knew she was in trouble.

He pulled her up from the deep dip with an exaggerated slowness that seemed to go on forever. Their eyes never left each other. As the music ended, he pulled her to him in a spin so that she was facing away from him--spoons on the dance floor, their arms crossed together over her body, his arm pressing into her breasts, his cock firmly nestled against her ass. Never before had she danced that hard, or that well.

His lips grazed her ear and landed with a warm, gentle caress on her neck. Her friends were sitting in their booth, eyes glued on them. Strangers clapped.

The music switched into a fast-paced Cha-cha and broke the mood. Dancers who'd stepped back to watch their Tango jumped back into action and the floor was crowded with people again.

Jerry steered her to the bar with his hand on the small of her back, searing hot against her naked skin. She ordered club soda. If she drank any more alcohol, she might not remember the magic. And tonight, was magical. She had almost convinced herself something like this would never happen.

The connection had been so personal, so close, so physical, she was certain she'd opened her insecurities and hopes to the entire room. She looked at him with new eyes. If dancing with him had been like this, what would happen if she got naked with him? Would she be able to stick to her own rules? *No. Nope. Nopety nope.* She would not let herself go down that line of thinking. There was no way she'd break her rules because of some dancing. *Only danger there.*

She shook her head. Granted, that Tango had been the sexiest dance she had ever had with anyone ever, but a single dance was not going to overcome years of dedication. She wanted more than that. She wanted a permanent thing. Jerry had said he'd be moving to D.C. soon, so maybe there would be time to develop this connection into something long-term.

They worked their way through the crowd back to the table and regrouped. It looked like the evening was coming toward a close. Katherine pulled the girls toward the bathroom for a quick conference.

"What do you think? All three back to Van's for an after party?"

Vanessa grinned. "Carl is kinda cute. I bet he's a virgin. I'll take him."

"What? You want to take his virginity? What kind of woman are you?" asked Katherine, with a jovial glance, knowing exactly what kind of woman Vanessa was.

"I've never had virgin sex. I'll bet it's super fun to take a guy like that. He's kind of like a puppy who's never been loved before."

"It's not. It's awkward and uncomfortable," Ashley said. "Besides I think Carl is way too young for you. And I doubt he's actually a virgin. He's too cute to have lasted this long."

"He's over twenty-one. Legal as far as I'm concerned." Vanessa crossed her arms. She was getting grumpy.

"There's more hype to it Vanessa, trust me, it's not worth it," said Ashley. "Besides, *guy*-virgins have no imagination and usually end up...you know...too early." She waved her hand vaguely in front of her.

"You mean they ejaculate quickly?" Katherine said, laughing. "It's not their fault. It's their first time, you know. It's a big deal. They just get over-excited."

Ashley laughed. "Just like a puppy."

"I think it's hysterical that I am the only one not fucking guys in this group, and I am the only one who can talk about sex without getting all tongue-tied." She paused and looked at Ashley. Her mind could get a little slow on martinis. "Wait a second. What do you mean about guy-virgins? As opposed to what? Girl-virgins?"

Vanessa's eyes went wide. "Of course. It's not like we didn't all know Ashley swings both ways...right?"

Katherine got the concept but didn't have any clue about Ashley. She turned to her, "Wait, you're bi? I had no idea."

"Seriously, Kitty-Kat? After all those times you saw me leaving Caroline Crawford's room?"

"I thought you were just close friends. You and Caroline were an item?"

"You didn't know? You're so worldly about every-thing, I can't believe it," Ashley shook her head. "I did like staying there, and we had lots of sex. Good sex. But, yeah. I have always enjoyed playing both teams."

Now that Ashley and Caroline's relationship was pointed out to her, she couldn't understand how she had missed it. She had always prided herself on how cool and calm and sedate she was when it came to all things sexual. How had she missed this?

"Anyway," Vanessa said, "Ashley, if you'll take Grant, I'll take Carl. We all know who's going to *not be fucking* poor Jerry boy tonight. He's going to have on a set of blue-balls."

Ashley shook her head. "Sorry, but I'm kinda going monogamous for a while."

This was news. Her beau back in Georgia must be stepping things up.

Carl groaned. He was looking downright sick. His skin had taken on a hue of green you don't see in the city very often. He'd hidden his insecurity and inability to hold a conversation by drinking heavily while others danced.

"I've got to go with him," Jerry explained to Katherine with a shrug. "He's my brother and I need to get him home." Even though she wanted more Tango-time with him, she had to give him props for not ditching his brother.

The guys declined Vanessa's offer of her limo, saying they would rather get Carl home without risking his barfing all over her car. Jerry and Grant hefted him out of the booth and carried him to a taxi instead.

The women watched as the cab pulled away. Katherine patted her purse. At least Jerry had her number.

They flopped into one row of the limo, leaning against each other all the way back to Vanessa's apartment. They dispersed to their own rooms for the night, Katherine wishing Carl hadn't gotten so drunk. She wanted to spend more time with Jerry.

Kat was not big into one night stands. She usually just danced and drank with the girls on these weekends, but, every once in a while, she'd been known to bring back a man to Vanessa's apartment. She only chose sober men and ones that were likely to be cool with just oral sex. A lot of guys actually preferred getting head because they didn't have to do anything. Katherine demanded satisfaction as well, and so far, she'd never been let down. At least not in the last five years or so. The only problem was finding a guy who was interested enough in hanging around more permanently. Even the best guys ended up wanting more than she was willing to give them.

She flopped onto her bed. She was wide awake with the memory of Jerry leading her body through the dance moves. She closed her eyes and pictured an alternate end to the evening. One where Jerry climbed into the limo with them and had come back with her.

She rolled onto her stomach, hand sliding between her legs and fingers roaming over her mound. She concentrated on that moment when they'd just finished the tango and he'd pulled her tightly against his chest, his cock pressing firmly against her ass, his lips hot against her neck.

Her fingers found her hungry, aching clit. She didn't need a slow, luxurious anything right now. She needed release, any release would do. She worked her fingers back and forth, fast and furious, her hips bucking against her hand. She moaned into her pillow as she came. It was a simple release from the sexual tension of the evening. She imagined his arms still wrapped around her as she went to sleep.

Chapter 5

The smell of coffee woke Katherine. She threw on a silk robe and found everyone in the kitchen already awake. No one was dressed except Lacy and Willow. They'd just flown in from Philly on Dexter's private plane. He had dropped them on his way to his family's place in Martha's Vineyard.

Lacy did well enough for herself with her career in advertising, but she wasn't into a life-long career of any kind. She was clearly ready to move on to the *Mrs. Dexter Stonesifer* stage of her life. He was already talking about when they'd be having their first offspring. Dex Jr. this and Dex. Jr. that. Katherine was happy for Lacy because marrying a rich man like Dex and pushing out his babies was exactly what she had said she wanted.

Katherine was excited for their wedding. They

were getting married at a private resort in Hawaii, and Kat had never been to Hawaii. While most people in their circle didn't have to think twice about the expense, Katherine had started saving the day Lacy and Dex had announced their engagement. Kat knew it was going to be a pricey deal, but she wouldn't back out of the Tri-Delt pledge to be there for her girl. The link to the turquoise and purple bridesmaids dresses Lacy had sent the previous week proved Katherine's theory about the ugliest dress competition.

Katherine loved the spa portion of her weekend. It was truly relaxing. They had no conversation, they all just relaxed in the ritual of having their hands and feet treated to excellent massages, lots of oils and lotions, and pretty colors on their nails. She could never get the polish to last a whole month, but she loved looking at her hands for a few days afterwards. There was something about having her nails all even and polished that made her feel more competent.

She'd need it the next week. She was leaving earlier on Sunday afternoon than usual to give her a few more hours in the office to make sure she had everything she needed done before work on Monday. It was her compromise to herself that let her come at all.

Katherine was just settling her feet into the hot warm bath of bubbles for her pedicure when her phone rang. She glanced at her purse hanging on the hook behind her. She would just ignore it. A few minutes went by, and it rang again. The woman working on her feet grabbed her bag for her and Kat dug into her purse for her phone. It was her mother. She looked at it as it rang a couple more times and slid her phone to off. She was in no mood to talk to her mom. She wanted to enjoy her weekend, and her mom only called when there was some drama or other involving one of her siblings. Kat had enough on her plate at the moment. She didn't need to get involved with anything else let alone giving her mother advice on how to deal with the latest. She'd call her back Monday. Or maybe Thursday after the hearings were over.

ON SATURDAY NIGHTS, the girls always went to a super-trendy restaurant that was at the top of some list or other--Zagat rated, fancy schmancy chef, a menu with ingredients she always got lost in the details, especially when the menu description was practically a small novel and things were served all foamed up or nitro'd into oblivion. The way the waiters at these places described the food as if it were literary fiction simply made her drool. She loved it. She loved that

Vanessa could get them into restaurants that usually had a six-month waiting list. Katherine never remembered their names because she just wanted the food, she didn't care what celebrity chef cooked.

Vanessa always paid for their Saturday dinners out. She planned the outing, made the reservations, sometimes months in advance, ordered the wine, and insisted everyone get four or five courses at each meal. Vanessa was a food blogger who penned often-scathing reviews of pretentious food in her spare time. People had made guesses about the *Bitch-Fork*'s identity, but only Vanessa and her sorority sisters knew she was the sarcastically hilarious voice behind the blog. Nobody ever thought a fantastically rich heiress would be a food blogger, it was the perfect secret identity.

They had to order as much food as possible so Vanessa could write about as many items on the menu as possible. She might flit around the table proclaiming she needed to eat a bite from every single plate or ask them to report on the food while taking copious notes. Was it overly salty? Was it boring and bland? How did it make you feel? Did you want to keel over and die or did you feel like you just experienced a private orgasm? Katherine figured the fact they never repeated a restaurant made it easier for Vanessa to conceal her identity.

The free food, even if sometimes pretentious, was

a definite perk of the weekend outings. And, frankly, it was almost always delicious even if sometimes ridiculous. Katherine didn't need 'rounds of venison served on pine needles on a slab of rough-hewn oak with huckleberry au jus, morel foam, and a dusting of fennel pollen' to be satisfied. But damn straight she would eat it and enjoy the dinner with no feelings of guilt whatsoever. She was helping out a friend, after all.

The lengths some people went to with food amazed her. Katherine's mom was a basic cook. Macaroni and cheese. Tuna casseroles. Spaghetti. Steak and potatoes. She had ten kids to feed, so there wasn't a lot of fuss or muss when it came to their kitchen. If her mom ever whisked something foamy, it was only by mistake.

The dinner tonight was at a place that she found slightly disconcerting. The interior was all white. White tables, chairs, walls, fixtures, dishes—even the silverware was white. It wasn't until her first plate arrived that she understood why. The bright red roasted pepper and asparagus were pure art on a plate.

She was just about to mess up the composition with her fork when her text alert dinged. Vanessa looked at her with utter disdain as she pulled her phone out of her purse.

"Sorry. I'll turn it to ignore after I check on this."

Kat held her phone under the table, aware that no one else in the restaurant had their phones out but her. She pointedly ignored the voicemail indicator. The only person who left voicemail was her mom. That could wait. Texts, on the other hand, usually mattered—it could be Carleen with some last-minute changes for the upcoming hearing.

It was Jerry. She couldn't help but feel out of breath, as if the very thought of his hands on her electrified her.

J: Where are you going tonight?

She gave him the address of the club and told him there were six women tonight. He promised to bring plenty of company so no one would feel left out. Last night had been the most perfect night she had ever had. She couldn't help but wonder if it was too good to be true, a one-off.

It was possible that Carl's 'getting sick' had been the guy-signal to ditch them, even though he did look pretty green around the gills. She hated the way she always second-guessed herself, but couldn't help it. Even though so many guys were cool with the no intercourse rule, none of them had stuck around either.

The waiter presented her second plate. Just a few minutes ago, Boudin Noir Aux Pommes had sounded delicious when Vanessa described it. But now, the notion of seeing Jerry again made her stomach jittery.

The thought of having two perfect nights of dancing was too much. She hadn't been sure he'd contact her again, and the text surprised her more than she wanted to admit. She tried to remain cool and collected, but inside, she wanted nothing more than to have him guide her through another Tango. Or Rhumba. It didn't really matter. Even a Cha-cha would do.

Chapter 6

They met up outside the club. It was one of those places with a roped-off line extending around the corner of the building. The rope kept people from filling in the sidewalk and creating a general mob around the entrance. The twenty-somethings in line were dressed to impress and entice. Two Goliath-sized bouncers in leather and sunglasses guarded the entrance. Kat never understood the sunglass at night thing, but she supposed it did give them a bad-ass appearance. As people approached, they were either let into the club or pointed to the end of the long line.

Jerry introduced his posse and Katherine introduced hers. The guys from the previous night had been augmented by men that were mostly older. Carl appeared to be the youngest in their group, and Vanessa made a beeline straight toward him.

She petted and cooed over him like he was her lost little puppy. Katherine had no doubt her friend would take him back to her apartment for some very adult lessons. If she had her way by the end of the night, Carl would walk out of her apartment either limping or a new man.

Jerry took her arm and led her to the entrance while the others auto-paired up and followed suit. Ashley linked up with the guy who looked the oldest in the group. Katherine couldn't hear what Jerry said to the bouncer, but, whatever it was, he got them all inside. They bypassed dozens of other people waiting in line. Vanessa tossed Katherine a look. She was clearly impressed. Usually, it was her influence that got them past the lines and into the clubs.

This club was louder and bouncier than the salsa club from the previous night. After half an hour of pulsing lights and booming music, Katherine felt a sudden warning pulse of doom in her head. She had had too much red wine, maybe. Something. She could hardly remember what she'd had at dinner. Once she'd gotten the text from Jerry, she'd eaten without thinking much about what was on her plate.

If she didn't get away from the flashing lights and booming noise soon, she'd be on her back with a migraine. She gave Vanessa a signal. Kat reached out for Jerry, but before she could say anything, he noticed that she was visibly upset and steered her into the VIP room, the bouncer recognized Jerry and let them pass by.

Another bonus about the man. He seemed to know her already. There were only a few people around, and they were all over by the bar. A waiter approached and directed Jerry to a quiet corner where there was an oversized chair and a large palm tree that gave them added privacy. Once in the VIP room, she explained that she needed a break from the music so her head didn't explode into bright stars and painful darts. Just removing herself from the noise, she was already feeling better. Knowing that Jerry would take care of her, helped relieve her anxiety.

"Thank you. I thought I was going to faint out there." The pounding had subsided and she was feeling almost like her normal self again.

He was suddenly close to her. His musky scent eviscerated the subtle pain, and she felt a new, different surge of energy.

"Are you sure you just want a break? Or was that an excuse to get me alone?"

She fell back against the wall, pulling her with him. "Having you here means I didn't have to drag one of them away from the fun with me."

"I want to kiss you, Katherine."

"I'm not going to stop you."

"What about your pending migraine?"

She closed her eyes and breathed in deeply. "I think we caught it just in time."

His lips were warm and soft. Just a simple kiss. The connection from the night before returned immediately. He pulled away, a question in his eyes. There was nothing shocking or incendiary about it. There were no sparkles clouding her vision, but it felt right.

Jerry shifted his weight and engulfed her in his arms, crushing her against him. One hand gently cradled her head, the other pulled her tight against him, pressing his erection against her stomach.

"I want you, all of you," he said. Before she could respond, his lips were on hers a second time.

This time, he didn't stop at a chaste peck. She invited him in, her mouth opening enough to let their tongues dance against each other. She roped her fingers through his hair, tugging at his curly locks.

An energy buzzed through her, an electric current that woke her, dissolved all vestiges of the headache, and made her insides hum.

Katherine had spent that last ten years hoping for this feeling while never actually expecting it. Treating it like some sort of fairy-tale that happened to other people, not her.

Last night, she had wanted to run from it. Tonight, she wanted to explore it. To tease out whatever meaning she could from it.

His hands slid along her bottom and along her thighs. He lifted her as though she weighed nothing to him. Her short skirt skid slid up her thighs. She wrapped her legs around his waist, allowing herself to enjoy the length of his hard cock through the bulk of his pants and her wet panties.

They kissed each other hungrily while clinging to each other, bracing themselves against the wall. His hard cock rubbed her through the fabric, rocking her, until he pulled his mouth away from hers, suddenly breaking that contact and leaving them each gasping for breath.

Had they come up for air, a pause? Things were happening way too fast, she almost forgot where they were. She released her legs and he helped her to the ground, but kept his arms around her waist. She wasn't about to tell him that she'd had the most mind-blowing kiss and full body clench she'd ever had in her entire life if he hadn't felt it, too.

"What?" she asked, pulling her skirt down, suddenly aware of other people in the room.

"Come with me to my hotel. You deserve more than a quickie," he said, his eyes roving over her body, as if it were already his, as if he knew exactly what she needed.

She placed a hand against his chest and searched his eyes. "I wasn't expecting any of this."

"This?" His eyes narrowed as he tilted his head toward her.

Hadn't he felt it?

"We need to slow down. That's all." Their kiss had escalated so quickly, she was afraid what might happen if she was alone with him in his room.

He rubbed a thumb against her lips and kissed her again. She ran her hands up his chest and linked her fingers behind his neck. She pulled him down for another long exploratory kiss.

The ravishing hunger kicked in, but Katherine reigned it in. Their hands explored each other through clothing, taking the measure of the other's bodies through cotton and lycra. He took his time when he found her breasts, teasing her nipples through the soft fabric until she was unable to stand on her own and let her body relax into his.

He lifted her in his arms and carried her over to one of the oversized chairs in the room, with a perfectly placed palm tree to give them privacy. He sat down with her on his lap without ever breaking the kiss. He slipped the sleeve of her dress off her shoulder and pulled her breast out of its skimpy cup. He sucked her nipple into his mouth, teasing it into a hard nub. She couldn't believe his audacity, but tilted her head back and moaned.

Just then, Vanessa came stumbling into the room with Carl attached to her arm. With a sudden movement, Jerry had pulled her sleeve back up to cover her and shifted her off his lap. Kat was pretty sure it was about getting caught or some old-fashioned sense of propriety. He jumped out of the chair and grabbed Carl by the arm, dragging him into the opposite corner.

Vanessa flopped onto the seat next to her. She was tipsy but not falling down drunk. "There you are. We're taking the limo home. I'll send it back for everyone else. I just wanted you to know. But....You look like you're having a good time. Maybe we should just stay here and join you." She placed her head against Kat's shoulder and blinked up at her.

"Come on Nessi," Kat gently pulled her to her feet. "You know I'm a one-on-one kinda gal. Are you sure you're okay going back with a guy? You're more than a little tipsy, you know?"

Vanessa blinked and her eyes cleared. "I'm good. He's cute. We're just going to have some fun."

Jerry and Carl had some quiet words Katherine couldn't catch, but when they came back, Carl held out his arm for Vanessa. They watched the couple leave, Carl guiding Vanessa like a gentleman escorting a lady into a ball.

"That's more like it," Jerry said. He pulled Katherine into his arms. "I just wanted to make sure Carl was sober enough to know if Vanessa is, you know...aware of what's going on."

"A lot of guys wouldn't care if their date was sloshed or sober."

A pained expression crossed his face. He adjusted his jacket and held out his arm to her. "We're not that kind of guy."

Katherine took his arm and leaned against him. There was something chivalrous about a man who looked out for other women. Gallant even.

"So," Jerry said. "How about a few more dances? If you're feeling up to it, that is."

She nodded and they headed to the dance floor. She looked back longingly at the sofa they'd just vacated. The club specialized in a basic electronic beat that sounded like an out of whack metronome. It was the kind of music that made their kind of dancing old-fashioned or retro. People here moved their arms and legs independently of each other or anyone else for that matter.

All she had to do was move her arms and hips to the beat of the music and people called it dancing, but she didn't care, as long as she was touching Jerry. He put his hand on her hip, and she shimmied into it. His eyes never left her, she might as well have been naked for all she knew. It was as though he was looking into her, not at her. Hot women surrounded him on all sides, yet he had eyes only for her.

Somehow the night got away from them, and they found their way to the front of the club. He leaned over and whispered in her ear, "I meant what I said."

She looked at him, not understanding. His eyes leveled to hers, but before he could clarify, Ashley appeared out of nowhere. She came between them, and threw her arms around Kat's shoulders almost knocking her off balance. "I've got to go home. You have to take me. Please come with me."

Her pupils were dilated, and it was clear there was something other than booze working on her.

"Ashley, honey, did you take anything?"

Ashley looked up at her, eyes bleary. "Just wine. Feels good though. Better than just wine kinda good."

Katherine did not want to leave, but there was no way she was going home with Jerry either. Ashley was barely able to keep her head up. Jerry gently pulled Ashley off Katherine and picked her up like a baby. He carried her outside and to the front of the taxi line. People made way for them when they saw Ashley lolling against Jerry's shoulder.

He tucked Ashley into the back seat of the cab

before turning back to Kat. "Make sure she gets home safely. I have your number."

You could come with us. But he couldn't read minds, could he?

Katherine was pissed at the asshole who'd roofied Ashley, but a small part of her was relieved she had an excuse to not go with him.

I have your number. How many times had she heard that before?

As she turned into the cab, Jerry placed a restraining hand on her upper arm. "You deserve more than a quickie." His green eyes bored into her. "I intend to keep that promise."

Chapter 7

*L*acy was already home when they arrived, and she helped Kat get Ashley settled into her room, propped on her side by pillows. Kat could hear the sounds of people having sex in the apartment—low voices murmuring, furniture thumping against the walls and floors. It took no imagination to figure out what was going on. Lacy had obviously heard it too, and turned the music up in the apartment.

I intend to keep that promise.

The words caused her heart to beat quickly. Why hadn't she asked Jerry to come with them after all? He'd already proved he was a gentleman twice over. She undressed in front of her mirror slowly, pretending she wasn't so alone. She peeled her dress off, pretending Jerry was watching her, revealing her underwear an inch at a time, practicing a slow strip-tease. Just as she was completely naked, Jerry texted her.

J: How's Ashley?

K: As bad as Carl last night.

J: I should have come with you.

K: I'm naked.

Katherine climbed into bed and propped herself comfortably on her pillows. There was a long pause before he answered. She was beginning to wonder if he would respond or if she had scared him off. He didn't seem like the kind of man who would frighten easily.

J: Okay. I'm naked now, too.

Katherine giggled. *That's* what had taken him so long.

K: Do you usually sleep naked?

J: All the time. I'd be a nudist if work would allow it.

Right.

K: You look pretty good in clothes. Do you have any tats?

J: Nope. You?

K: Yes. One.

J: Show me.

Kat glanced at the tat on her inner thigh and considered how she could best take a photo of it. Show him too much at once, and there was no mystery. She angled the camera so it barely showed the top of her mound, a narrow wedge of pubic hair daintily pointing the right direction. The tat was an artistic rendition of three triangles combined into a cool looking design, entwining the triangles into something Celtic. All the Tri-Delts in her year had the same tat, all in the same place.

J: Interesting.

Now, what exactly did that mean? Was he being judgy? She hated not being able to hear inflections.

K: Why don't you call me. Texting one handed is awkward.

Her phone buzzed in record time.

"So, how does this work?" he asked.

"You've really never talked to anyone while getting off before?"

"Not over the phone."

"Okay. I'm sure you'll get the hang of it." She adjusted herself so she was comfortable. "Are you on your bed?"

"Yeah. I'm um, kind of lounging."

"Well, we can either imagine we are in the same room together and tell each other what we would like to be doing, or we can masturbate at the same time and describe it."

"You mean like I tell you I'm lying back on my bed thinking about you, and I'm as hard as I've been for any woman?"

"That's a good start, but what's so hard, *exactly*?" she asked, teasing him.

"Oh, I see. Specifics are important, eh?" He cleared his throat and chuckled. "Okay then. My cock is fully erect and wanting attention."

"There we go," she said. "You're a quick learner."

"Are you wet?"

"I don't know, let me check." She was throbbing. If she touched herself just the right way, she'd come. She wasn't ready for that. Not yet. "I'm putting you on speaker phone so I can use both hands. My left hand is twisting my left nipple while my other hand is checking to see how wet I am."

"Details, woman."

"I'm gliding my fingers across my belly. I don't touch myself where I want to be touched—yet. Instead, I'm caressing my inner thigh, tracing the tattoo slowly. I'm teasing myself, but carefully. My pussy is throbbing for you. I'm pretty sure I'll come quickly tonight."

"Don't touch your clit. Pull your outer lips open and finger yourself to see how wet you are."

Katherine did as he suggested. Her fingers came

out shiny and slick with her juices. "I'm dripping with excitement. I'm overflowing and dripping down my butt crack."

"If I were with you..." he growled.

"You'd what? What would you do if you were with me right this second?" she asked, knowing he could say anything he wanted because they were miles away from each other.

"I'd bury my face in your pussy."

She sighed in relief. "I lift my fingers to my mouth, tasting myself."

"Holy fuck, Katherine. I want to be with you so bad."

"We're together, in a way."

"My hand is wrapped around my cock, I'm stroking myself."

"I'm putting two fingers in my pussy now, finger fucking myself."

"Do you like giving head?" he asked.

She hmmed in response, *he had no idea.* "Do you like eating pussy?"

Another low groan. She could hear his hand moving up and down his shaft. "You're really going at it, aren't you?"

"Of course I am." His breathing had quickened.

She spread her legs open and found her throbbing clit.

"I can't wait to taste you. Make you scream in delight. Have you begging me to stop."

"I can't wait to feel your tongue on my pussy."

"I'm picturing your lips wrapped around my cock...Come for me, Katherine. I want to hear you when you come."

"Yes," she said. "I've got two fingers on my clit, pretending it's your tongue driving me crazy." She wanted to feel his lips on her mouth. On her breast. On her thigh. On her wet mound.

She moved her fingers fast and furious against her clit.

"Come for me, Katherine," he said, his voice dissolving into a grunt followed by a satisfied sounding moan.

She pictured his cock erupting across his hand and flat stomach. She wasn't shy when it came to making noise, so she didn't hold back. She was pretty sure everyone in the apartment could hear her screaming in delight.

When they both finished, she picked up the phone and could hear him still breathing heavily.

"Wow," he said. "I had no idea phone sex could be so hot. Imagine what we could do to each other if we were actually in the same room."

She chuckled. "Oh, believe me. I am."

"I meant what I said earlier, Katherine."

"About what?" she asked. She stretched across the bed, wishing she was snuggling into his broad chest.

"About you deserving more than a quickie."

"Is this move to D.C. a done deal?"

"It wasn't. But, I think I'll make it one now."

Katherine usually stayed in New York until midnight on Sunday, returning home for minimal sleep before work on Mondays. She changed her plans and returned to D.C. early. She wanted to spend Sunday afternoon working. That was what she told herself, but she couldn't help feeling like she was trying to get out of New York. She wanted to shake the unsteady feeling she'd had since she met Jerry, and get herself under control. The office was empty, and she managed to get a solid eight hours of work done without any interruptions.

She went home at midnight and got up at five to do her usual early morning run with Kenny, her running buddy for their usual Monday routine. Kenny was full of his own weekend stories, except he couldn't tell her who he had been working for, of course. He was one of D.C.'s professional fixers who swept in to save various public figures and their families from scandal. He'd spent the entire weekend covering up for *someone* whose teenage son had driven his car into a pool Friday night. No one was hurt, but the son had already had his licensed yanked for a DUI and wasn't supposed to be driving. Kat was pretty sure if she scoured the internet she would find no hint of the episode anywhere.

"I swear. The internet is making my job easier and harder at the same time. You throw enough ridiculous made up shit out there, and people stop believing anything," he said after explaining how they got the Land Rover out of the pool without anyone leaking the drama. "Enough about boring drunk people who don't know how to drive. How was your New York weekend?"

"It was unbelievable."

Kenny slowed to a jog. "I'm pretty sure you've never used that adjective when referring to one of your girl weekends."

"Nope. I never have. I was actually scared out of my wits. I was practically fucking a guy against a wall, and a small part of me thought I might...MIGHT...just let him."

Kenny stopped running. "Why didn't you tell me when we could have a martini? This is ridiculous Kitty-Kat, now I have to listen to this amazing story without any alcohol. Are you trying to kill me?"

Kat tried to explain the strange sensation that had overwhelmed her. The way things had gone all fuzzy around her vision, the way everything had slowed down around them, the connection. How she had wanted to savor it and run away at the same time. How he danced so perfectly, and when he brought her in close, she wanted to just take him right there on the dance floor.

"You know what that's called, don't you Kat?"

"I've never had it happen before."

"Let me spell it out for you sister. It's called L.O.V.E. What are you going to do about it?"

"What can I do?"

"Find him, bend over and let him fuck you till the sun comes up."

Katherine laughed. Fucking was Kenny's answer to everything. "Right. You know my rules dude."

"And I will never, ever understand them. So, does this Adonis have a name?" He started back up with their run.

"Ugh. That's the only problem. His name is Jerry."

Kenny tossed her a withering glare. "I cannot believe you sometimes. I'd get it if he were an Adolph or a Donald...that would be pretty hard to get over. But there is nothing wrong with the name *Jerry*." He made his eyes wide and innocent looking and shifted his voice into an approximation of her sultry alto. "*Jerry. Oh, OH my god Jerry! Take me now Jerry. Fuck me wild Jerry!* See? Nothing wrong with the name. Would you like to try?"

Kat laughed. "It just seemed wrong for him. He was standing there looking so...so...tall and broad and basically god-like. He's better looking than you are."

Kenny shot her an over-the-top fake astonished look. "No. How can that be? So, Jerry what? What's his last name? I have to see what he looks like. I'm doing a full background."

"I have no idea."

"You find a guy who makes you tremble all over, a guy who dances like Astaire, a guy who makes you *even think* about fucking him and you don't get his whole name?"

"I have his number, he has mine."

"And have you texted him back?"

"Well, we kinda had phone sex Saturday night."

"Kinda? Good lord, girl. How do you kinda have phone sex? You either did or you didn't."

"We both got off, if that's what you're asking."

"Did you facetime? Or was it just voice?"

"Just voice."

"So, you're not doing that stupid three-day rule thing are you?"

Kat backhanded Kenny's bicep with a light grunt. "I just thought it would be better to wait since he said he'd text me. It's only been since late Saturday night. Besides, I want to see if he really likes me. I need to know that."

"Text him. Tell him you're thinking about him. Games backfire in the end, you know that. Text me his phone number, and I'll run a background. Make sure he's not some whacked out serial killer."

"I'll send you the info later today. I don't think you need to do a background on him, though..."

"You know I do backgrounds on everyone you go out with. And, I want you to stop the silly Jerry nonsense, 'kay?"

"Okay, okay fine. See you tomorrow, honey." They split at their regular spot. Katherine slowed her jog to a walking cool-down.

She didn't think Jerry was a player. The way he'd checked in with Carl about Vanessa being drunk, the way he'd scooped up poor Ashley? Those weren't the kinds of things a player does. No, he had a genuine aura surrounding him.

He had already texted her in New York. Hell, they'd had phone sex. He definitely had her number and knew how to use it. Was he going to text her again? Sometime. When he got around to it. But, seriously, how much time does it take to text something. Anything? Hello? Maybe the phone sex had actually been too much. But he was the one who said she deserved more than a quickie.

She closed her eyes and pictured him in front of her, remembered how he felt as he pressed himself against her. By the time she got home, she was breathing hard. And not just from running. She spent the time in the shower imagining his hands moving up and down her soap slathered skin, bringing herself to a climax. *Damn that was fast.* She got dressed wondering where he was, what he was doing. He had said he was moving to D.C. soon. How soon?

It was only Monday. Rather than going all high-school and worry about him, she'd focus on work and BINGO. She had a huge hearing in less than two days and a BINGO game to win.

Her connection at the CIA hadn't gotten back to her yet, and she hadn't come up with another winning scenario on her Bingo card. Two more slots. CIA and Lobbyist. That's all she needed to win. She had four more days, she'd make it work out. She scoured Instagram for check-ins from people playing the BINGO game. Her only real competition looked like Madeline. Cheyenne was a close second. She still had a fighting chance.

If she was going to have a chance at winning this trip, she'd better get on the ball. While she wanted Jerry to call her back, she didn't know if he would. And she wasn't the kind of girl who was going to wait around the phone to see if he called. She had a game to win.

The Congressman was involved in an upcoming hearing that would discuss and draw out the pros and cons of an environmental issue. Her job was to make sure that the hearing went smoothly, that the questions were on target, and that the experts called to task stayed on task. She had two days of preparation hell before the hearing began. She expected it to go quickly. She was pretty sure that the only reason for the hearing was so that certain members of Congress could get their faces on cameras looking serious about a cause everyone pretty much agrees upon. It would make for good press, something everyone needed more of lately.

Carleen tapped at her door half-way through the morning. "Got some info on the hearings for you."

The older woman looked tired. She'd been

Lincoln's right-hand woman for ten years, ever since he'd been in the state legislature. She'd followed him to D.C. to ensure a smooth transition and stayed. Her decision had eventually ended her marriage of twenty-five years. Her ex hated D.C. and finally divorced her to move back home.

If it weren't for Carleen, Katherine wouldn't even have a job here. She was her boss, a mentor, and a long-time family friend. They down-played that last bit in the office because nepotism never looked good, and perception is everything. And it wasn't exactly nepotism.

Kat's father and Lincoln Pierce had worked in the same law practice together. While Kat's dad was a career attorney, Link had left the practice in his thirties to pursue politics. The break had been amicable even though Pierce had taken Carleen from the practice. None of that mattered though. The truth was Kat had earned her spot fair and square with an excellent work ethic and track record. She was secure in her professional life—both her competency and accomplishments. Maybe not so much when it came to men.

Carleen slid a folder across the desk. "We have a list of new people who will be testifying from Walker's office."

Katherine flipped it open. Three names and a brief synopsis of their job descriptions at the think tank

CGF--Colman Greyson and Franks. CGF had a reputation as an objective firm that did good environmental work. "Carleen, there's nothing here but a list of names. Marcus Griffin, Gerard Porter, Grant Tanner. Are we running backgrounds on any of these people?"

Carleen laughed a harsh this-is-not-funny laugh. "We just got the list a couple of hours ago. I'm putting a rush on it. But, we have no idea how these guys are going to affect the hearings until they're actually testifying."

"Should I see if Kenny can do a background on them? He might not have the same...erm...hurdles to jump through as we do."

Carleen sucked in her lower lip as she considered the possibilities. "I don't really want to take the chance of anything sketchy tipping them off."

"Right. You know, Carleen, CGF would only bring good science to the table. Heck, we considered hiring them to do our evaluation of the project, so I don't think they would possibly hurt us. I just don't understand Walker's motivation for bringing them in, or why he'd hand over this list so late."

"Those are my concerns, exactly." She stood in Kat's doorway for a few minutes as they brainstormed a few scenarios. Nothing that bad came to the surface though, at least nothing that could harm them on Wednesday during the hearing. Walker was a slime-bucket through and through, but he couldn't openly go against this legislation. It would be political suicide.

Kat delved back into work and was relieved to be closing the file early enough so she could get home and order in some Thai. The long party nights on the weekend were catching up with her. She'd order in some satay and noodles and relax in a hot bubble bath with a book and a glass of wine. When was the last time she'd settled into a good book? She'd unwind in blessed solitude.

All she wanted was to go home. She was close to burning out, and didn't feel like going out with anyone. She wasn't sure she'd even go out with Jerry right that second. What was wrong with her. Jerry. Jerry. Jerry. Jerry. She could get used to the name. All she had to do was use some positive imaging. Tall Adonis of a man. That lock of curly dark hair falling over his forehead. Those green eyes. His strong hands with fingers strong enough to satisfy her every need.

She was about to wrap up her day, when Harrison showed up. Katherine quickly considered and dismissed him as a possible kiss. For a brief moment, she tuned out Harrison while thinking of her BINGO card. She had to kiss a lobbyist to win the BINGO game, and that was the problem, she couldn't imagine any circumstances where she'd want to get that close to a lobbyist.

Katherine adjusted her expression to a poker face and hoped he didn't realize what she was thinking about. She still thought he was handsome but since she had met Jerry, the idea of being with anyone else had simply vanished. He wanted to discuss Chloe and the various problems that had arisen with their favorite problem: Gordy the lobbyist was close to uncovering their plans for the meeting in Vegas.

The only way to get Gordy off their back was to present him with a situation that was believable. Kat could see that Harrison liked Chloe a lot and suggested to Harrison that he should date Chloe. She trusted Harrison. He wouldn't play with her or go too far with the charade. He was one of the good guys.

Kat did what she had to do. If there was no Sunflower, there was no reason to even play BINGO. She believed in this legislation and wanted to make sure nothing tanked it. Especially not a bozo of a lobbyist sticking his nose in where it didn't belong.

Chapter 10

*K*at stopped mid-stride, mail in hand, staring at her front door. The entry way light was on, and she was certain she'd turned it off before leaving in the morning. She approached her door slowly. She had locked it. With the bolt. She turned the knob slowly and pushed. The door swung open on squeaky hinges so she kicked the door wide open.

"I'm calling the police. If you're still here, you better get out now."

She swiped at her phone with shaky fingers. She'd never been burgled before.

"What in the world? Katherine Agatha Joan O'Malley? Why in the world would you call the police on your mother?"

Katherine stopped swiping and stepped inside.

Her mom was coming out of the kitchen wiping her hands on a towel.

"Mom? What are you doing here?"

"I'm almost done making dinner. I don't understand how a person can live without food in their refrigerator. Sweetheart, a head of lettuce and a few condiments? Honestly, what do you live on? I bought a good week's worth of groceries."

The spicy smell of tangy garlic, tomatoes, and basil filled the air. Katherine was unaccustomed to the smell of something cooking in her kitchen. She avoided it at all costs, and rarely heated anything other than what she could fit in the microwave. The last thing she wanted to do on a weekend was clean a dirty kitchen. She'd cleaned up after her mother plenty of times as a kid, she didn't want to do it now.

"I didn't mean that, not cooking. I meant, why are you here. In D.C.?"

"Well, not that you answered any of my calls, did you?"

Katherine glanced uneasily at the answering machine. Then she remembered the ignored messages from the weekend. She'd completely spaced on them. "Oh...Mom, I'm sorry. I was busy when you called and then totally forgot."

She shut the door and followed her mother into the kitchen, noting that her apartment had been transformed in the course of the day. Her mother had done the laundry and sorted the mail. Every single inch of her little brownstone had been vacuumed and dusted. She could run a gloved finger over any horizontal space and come up clean. The truth was, she was a bit surprised. Growing up, her mother had a hard time keeping up the house and it usually came down to her. It had impacted her life in so many ways. Not only did she not want kids, she didn't want to cook or clean. Katherine had been meaning to get a maid, she'd just been too busy to call and hire a service.

The kitchen was spotless, even though she must have made a mess preparing whatever was in the oven. The table was set for two. Katherine was pretty sure the dishes on the table belonged to her, but since she ate primarily out of take-out containers she couldn't be entirely certain.

"Mom?"

Her mother opened the oven door and peeked inside, closing it before Katherine could see what was cooking. She had to admit, she was hoping it was lasagna. Her mom made excellent lasagna. A bowl filled with salad greens filled her with hope. While she loved Thai take-out, it was not nearly as good as her mom's pasta.

"I left your father."

Her mother left her father once a year. At least.

Katherine's heart rate had slowed down from the burglary scare. This was not new. She didn't try to talk her out of it. She'd stopped trying at least three years ago. Nope, the new routine was to just treat her mom like she was here to stay and make plans to help her move in.

After a week, her mom would be tired of the ruse and go back home. The more Katherine tried to get rid of her mom, the harder it was to actually do that. Instead, she had found reverse psychology had worked wonders.

"Okay. Okay. I'm sorry to hear that. Did you get your suitcase to the guest room...I mean...your room okay?"

"Of course I did honey. Now, you go get changed for dinner. I don't want you spilling red sauce on that lovely blouse." She leaned in closer to look at Katherine's shirt. "Is that silk? You know that costs money to dry clean."

"Yes, it is. And you are absolutely right about that. I will go throw on something more lasagna appropriate."

As soon as Katherine was alone in her bedroom, she called her sister. "Margaret, what the hell? Why didn't you tell me she was upset with Dad again? She's at my house."

Her sister cackled. "You didn't ask. You really should answer your phone more often."

"You didn't call me. Mom called me and didn't leave a message. How was I supposed to know something was going on?"

"Mom totally hit the wall and freaked out."

"But, why didn't you keep her with you. It's your turn, anyway."

"You know it doesn't work like that."

"You have the kids. The life to distract her. When she's here, she's alone ALL day. And the only thing she does is cook and clean. My apartment looks like it's ready for the cover of Architectural Digest, and I swear that lasagna in the oven will feed us for two weeks. I knew I should have gotten a roommate. Then I wouldn't have a guest bedroom."

"Oh, boo-hoo. Poor Katherine has Mommy cooking her dinner."

Katherine shrugged out of her blouse, changing while still on the phone. "I have the biggest hearing of my career coming up in two days. TWO DAYS? I have dates planned. I cannot host Mom all week. This is nuts. When is Dad coming to get her? Please tell me he's on his way."

"Ooooooh nooooo, Kat. This time is different. Dad isn't coming for her this time."

Katherine dropped onto the bed. Her mom went off the rails and ran off to one of her children's homes every so often. She tended toward Katherine's because she was one of her ten children who was unmarried. For whatever reason, that made her feel the most useful. She could cook, clean, and nag ... not necessarily in that order.

She could be the perfect housewife before Dad would get in the car and drive from Chicago to pick her up. It was a predictable vacation of sorts—not that her mom ever took a real vacation and called it that. Maybe she couldn't let herself take one without the drama. There was always some huge fight or blow-up between her parents to use as an excuse.

"What do you mean, he's not coming?" Katherine asked, all the bluster out of her. This couldn't be happening.

"They had a huge blow-out fight. I wasn't there, but Joan was home. And, she said that Mom was actually throwing pottery. The pieces that Dad bought her for one of their anniversaries—you know the ones from Bennington?"

Katherine's chest tightened. Could someone her age have a heart attack? An overwhelming sense of dread weighed down on her. "Mom was throwing pottery? At Dad?"

Her mom was not prone to throwing anything, let alone expensive pottery that would crash into the wall and make a mess she would end up cleaning up. Violence and making messes were not her thing. She loved the dark green stoneware—she had to be really upset to break any of it.

"I know, sounds crazy, right?" There was a wailing sound over the other end. "Hold on sweetie. Bonnie's needing me."

The wailing grew louder, and Kat heard the phone shuffle around as Margaret picked up her youngest and cooed at her. Bonnie settled down right away.

"All right. She's latched on nicely. Where were we?"

Katherine pictured her sister settling down into the old family rocking chair her dad had refinished when Margaret had announced her first pregnancy. She had only seen Bonnie once since she'd been born. "Can you switch to face-time so I can see her?" Kat asked.

"Kat, I'm nursing. You won't see much but my boob."

"Okay, fine. I really ought to come out for a visit sometime soon. She's probably getting so big by now." Kat turned to the row of photos on her dresser. Front and center were photos of the youngest of the O'Malley clan. In one, Bonnie lay on her back with her toes reaching almost to her chin as her hands grabbed onto them, her face a cherubic grin. Kat traced the big grin on her niece's sweet face.

"She's sitting up and showing signs of crawling

already. Keeping up with her big brother is a tough job."

"I bet. I swear I'll fly out there before the end of the summer. So.... Back to Mom and Dad. Any idea why Mom is here this time?"

There was a long pause. Margaret's quiet was unsettling. "Katherine. It's about another woman. It's not the usual kind of thing."

Chapter 11

After dinner, Kat point blank asked her mom what was going on with her and Dad. She asked if there was another woman. Mom lifted her apron to her face and ran crying from the kitchen. She'd locked herself in her room and wouldn't come out for the rest of the night.

Katherine didn't know what to do, so she cleaned up the kitchen and put away the left overs. Again, she was the one in charge of helping her mother, taking care of her. She tried knocking on the door again, and when she didn't answer, decided to go to bed. Why couldn't her mom grow up and be a normal mom?

The next morning, Kat woke up tired. The lasagna from the night before sat like a ball in her stomach. Sleep had come in fits and bits. Either the situation with her parents was getting to her or it was the heavily cheesed delicious and decadent pasta that her body wasn't used to.

When she got back from her morning run, her super-cheery-no-problems-ever mom had made her waffles, bacon and coffee for breakfast. She shook her head. First, she wouldn't speak to her, and now she was trying to apologize with a giant breakfast. No wonder they were all so fucked up. Katherine skipped the waffles, and explained to her mom that the sugar would cause her to crash. Even so, she would have to go on another run at lunch to make up for all the food her mother was pushing at her.

She gave her mom her extra metro pass and suggested she go to the Smithsonian for a visiting exhibit that Cheyenne waxed poetical about over coffee the previous day. Who knew Chey would suddenly develop a thing for ancient Persian pottery? It wasn't until she'd mentioned it that she thought of her mother's own beloved pottery in shards. What was she going to do? Should she call up Dad and beg him to come get her? She didn't want to. They had a good relationship, but they weren't that close.

Once on the train into work, Kat was afraid her mom might show up at the office. She texted her a list of other things she could see in D.C. There was a new exhibit opening at the art museum. Maybe she could go to the arboretum. At least this year's time-out was during the height of the Cherry Blossom Festival. Jerry had told her about a new exhibit Neil deGrasse Tyson had designed at the air and space museum.

The memory of dancing with Jerry popped up in her mind, and her body shuddered in delighted response. If she closed her eyes, she could almost smell him and feel his fingers spinning her around the dance floor. That he had seemed confused about her response to their kiss made her think he hadn't felt the same way. If he had, wouldn't he have texted or called by now?

She looked through her settings to make sure her phone was working, but she had plenty of texts from the homeland security guy and a couple from reporter guy, the two guys she had dated last week, but wasn't interested in. And, why hadn't Kenny texted back yet? How long did it take to run a background check? She hoped it was nothing bad.

She tried to not focus on Jerry. Maybe he was a player, and she had just been another fun night out on the town, so she focused on her work. Carleen came into her office first thing, and they ran through all the documentation one more time. The background checks on the new witnesses would be done before the hearing. It wasn't a huge deal, but at least she would have a few minutes in the morning to take a quick look at them. Before she knew it, Carleen was headed out and on her way to another meeting.

The science would come down on their side, of that she was sure. Thinking about science distracted her from work again. She bit her lip and wished she'd taken a picture of him. God he was hot, that strong jawline. The way he led her around the dance floor. He had said he was moving to DC, but she couldn't help but wonder when. She chided herself for being so silly. He was probably one of those guys. She had probably misread him.

Still, it had been less than a one-night stand. Two nights of dancing. His hands on her hips. The way he looked at her. And the searing, sexy kisses against the club wall, the way his hard dick rubbed against her. And phone sex didn't really count. They had never gotten naked together. Not in person anyway.

She shoved away the circular thoughts and got back to work. What was she going to do? Masturbate in the bathroom? Just as she had finally cleared her head, Cheyenne came into her office holding a plate with a delicious looking pastry on it. She pushed it slowly across the desk toward Katherine.

Katherine leaned over and inhaled the warm cinnamony sweetness. Cheyenne was the most incredible baker she'd ever met, and she was constantly bringing in her experiments.

"I'm worried about what Carleen will do when she finds out about this whole Bingo thing," said Cheyenne.

"She'll be pissed. Tells us to quit. Make some threats about firing us." She pulled a corner edge off the pastry. A dark brown glaze pooled out onto the plate. She dipped the dough into the glaze and ate it. The rich caramel and yeasty dough was balanced by the cinnamon and a hint of salt. "What do you call this one? It's like a cinnamon roll, but also kind of like a pop-tart. You could make a killing selling these, you know that right?"

Cheyenne's face clouded. "Making pastries is not in service to the greater good." Her voice had dropped into a low monotone. Like she was repeating a mantra. She shook her head before continuing. "Anyways. You think Madeline is playing fair with this one?"

"She came up with the idea pretty damn fast."

"I was thinking the same thing. But," Cheyenne leaned forward stretching across the desk, "I'll tell you one thing. I'm having a shit-ton of fun. I swear, this game got me thinking outside the box."

Cheyenne shifted gears, she ran a neatly mani-cured fingernail along the top of Katherine's desk. "Hey, do you think Opal is cool with this? She hardly said anything when we were setting up the game, and she hasn't claimed any scores on her card yet."

"Opal is the silent one who won't rock the boat. She's not going to drag Carleen into this, regardless of whether she's playing or not. I haven't seen her do any Instagram check-ins, so I don't think she's actively playing."

"I don't think she is either. Can you imagine working here for nearly ten years and still being whatever her title is?"

"Opal is dedicated to the Congressman, probably to a fault and clearly as a detriment to her own career. She never plays to win anything for herself."

"I think she's in love with the Congressman."

Katherine had never considered Opal as a romantic interest for the Congressman. "Aren't we all in love with him at some level? How else you could explain the general level of commitment in this office."

"Don't get me wrong, but I think that kind of blind adoration is problematic in the long run. That kind of devotion leads to cover-ups and scandal."

Katherine's attention was diverted by an email alert. It was from her friend who worked in the CIA. "Speaking of the game..." She held a finger up to Cheyenne, silently asking her to wait before saying anything and opened the email.

Her friend had set her up with a guy named Ryan Devlin. She sent a picture too. Buff with what she was sure a six-pack under his shirt, a cleanly shaven face, short, military hair, and a Holy-moly body. Her jaw must have dropped open because Cheyenne was up out of her seat and looking over her shoulder before she could click the email closed.

"Oh. My. Fucking. GOD. He's a god. Totally...Is this a guy for the game?" Cheyenne asked, practically drooling onto Katherine's shoulder.

"CIA."

"Hey, I need a CIA guy. Would you lend him to me when you're done?"

"Why would I help you win?"

"To keep Eleanor or Madeline from winning. That's why."

"I don't think so. Looks like I have a date tomorrow night, after the hearing."

"Don't try so hard Kat. I recognize the sound of fake happiness. I'll go if you're not into him."

Kat drummed her fingers on the desk. "Okay. So...I met this guy in New York. It feels strange to date someone while I'm waiting to hear from another man."

"You are such a good girl Katherine. Someone from the game?"

"Actually no. That's what makes this timing so terrible. New York guy can dance. I mean, *my style,* old-fashioned ballroom dancing. Tango. Rumba. He's incredible." Katherine closed her eyes and she was back in the Latin club tangoing with Jerry again. His touch. A hot longing filled her, and all she wanted was to feel his lips on hers, his hands on her body as they glided across a dance floor.

"Woah, you look like you need some private time. Should I go?"

Katherine flushed, opening her eyes to see Cheyenne looking at her with a huge grin. "I thought we had a connection, but he hasn't texted or called."

"Yeah. Well, definitely time to cut bait and move on if you want to win this thing."

"I was just kind of hoping for...something..."

"We're all hoping for that something, Katherine. But, you don't owe Mr. New-York-guy anything. Unless he calls you again, I don't get why you wouldn't go after the awesomeness that is this CIA guy."

Katherine took another look at Ryan Devlin. "Yeah. He's good looking. I wonder what he does." She read her friend's email. "All she says is, he works for the CIA and that's all she can tell me. Funny. He probably works in the mail room."

"Not with that chin. Man. He's like James Bond meets Abercrombie and Fitch. Besides, it doesn't matter what he does, it only matters that he works for the CIA."

"It was just a kiss. No use giving up on the game, eh?"

"That a girl. And, when you're done with him,

please, oh, please, pass him on to me? He's like my wet-dream."

"Oh, thanks, Cheyenne. Now I'm going to go out with him knowing that? Ugh."

"Just a kiss? Yeah, I guess that's the minimum requirement, right?"

"Cheyenne, you're incorrigible!"

"No. I'm just a modern woman."

"Are you sleeping with these guys?"

"Oh, no. There is no sleeping involved, Katherine."

"Whatever. Just keep it safe, right?" Katherine liked Cheyenne's spring-like energy and constant buoyancy. She had a natural resiliency that Kat admired.

Cheyenne was quick to take the hint. "No, but be sure to let me know when you're ready to hand that CIA stud over to me. Kind of jealous you will be going out with him first."

"My friend, my find."

Katherine checked her phone. Maybe Jerry had texted and she hadn't noticed. There was nothing from him. Katherine emailed her friend to set up the date.

Chapter 12

Katherine went straight to the gym after work. If she didn't, her mother's food was going to overwhelm her slight frame. She wouldn't be able to work out enough to keep up with the calories, but she could try.

Her audio books were a prime workout diversion. She could spend hours on a treadmill as long as she had something to keep her occupied. She drifted off into a high-fantasy-romance--elves and dwarves and knights fighting on the side of good and justice by day and blowing off steam with amazing sex at night.

The main character had been a nebulously good looking guy in her head, but as she upped the speed on the treadmill, she realized that she had replaced the fuzzy image with Jerry's.

After an hour, her audiobook's auto timer shut it off, and she reluctantly returned to reality. She wiped the sweat running off her face with a towel and headed to the weights. She could get in a quick upper body set and be home before her mother had a fit. She had texted twice already. While scrolling to find her mom's name in the contact list, she saw Jerry's name.

She clicked his name, her finger hovering over the delete contact button, but a quiet panic hit her. If she did that, there would be no way to contact him or figure out who he is. Instead, she texted Kenny to see where he was on that background check. Maybe he'd found something bad and been debating whether to tell her or not. It would be just like Kenny to withhold information from her.

She had just finished a couple of sets of bicep curls when she saw something out of the corner of her eye. It was not exactly that she saw something so much as felt it-- a familiar presence.

She turned slowly, and there, not twenty feet away, was Jerry, spotting someone doing chest presses. He was in a more modest muscle shirt than a lot of guys wore in the gym, but he was showing more skin than she had seen the entire weekend. He wasn't bulky like a lot of the gym rats, but he was firm and sculpted.

She expected his partner to be a man, but long hair draped over the edge of the bench and almost hit the floor on either side. He was spotting for a woman. Katherine couldn't make out her facial features, but she could tell she was a gym bunny. Her arms were firm, maybe a little on the bulgy side of feminine.

Jerry was concentrating on the task at hand-- keeping a couple hundred pounds from crushing the woman's mostly flat chest. Katherine counted the plates again. Sure enough, there were two fifties on each side of the bar along with a few twenty and ten pounders. Damn. Strong woman.

Katherine did a lat pull-down thinking maybe she could mosey on over to Jerry after he was done helping wonder woman. Except she didn't just do one set. After she'd done six killer looking lifts, Jerry moved fifty pounds off each side and the woman did some quick lifts with the lighter weight. He hovered over her, clearly interested in making sure she was okay, even though it looked like she had no problem with a hundred pounds removed.

Katherine finished a second set of lats about the same time it looked like they were done. Kenny was right. Game-playing always ended in disaster. She should just walk over to him and say hello. Her heart started beating at the thought of it. What would she say? *Fancy meeting you here. Long time no see. Lose your phone?*

She started towards him. The woman snaked her

arms around Jerry's neck and kissed him full on the mouth, pressing her body full up against his. This was not a little chaste friendly, thanks for spotting me peck on the cheek.

He placed his hands on the woman's biceps, so it wasn't exactly a hot embrace, but he wasn't jumping away either. They were at the gym after all. Either they were a couple, or Jerry had women everywhere he went.

This couldn't be right. He had asked Katherine if she believed in love at first sight. They had something special. He had felt it, too, didn't he? Had she actually believed that love would happen to her? She bit her lip so hard, it left a painful sting. Had she been suckered by a cheesy line?

Jerry looked over in her direction. His eyes rounded in surprise before glancing down at the woman in his arms. He had that look of being caught in a lie. He had her number, and he hadn't used it. He was kissing another woman instead.

Katherine spun on her heel and raced out of the gym. She was outside, down the block, and almost on the subway before she realized she'd left her clothes and purse in her locker. The gym was closer to work than home. She had no money. Her metro pass was in her locker. Her work credentials were there, too. It would be a total pain to come back to the gym before work in the morning. She was so angry, that she seri-ously considered walking the four miles back to her apartment, but there was no way she was walking home--it was pouring rain outside. She had to go back inside.

Chapter 13

*S*he stood in front of the gym and took a deep breath. How had she missed him? She'd had her audio book on, picturing him running around as the protagonist of her novel for a whole hour when he'd been just a few feet away. It wasn't that bad. She could sneak behind the leg machines. If she could get to the pool unnoticed, she could get to the women's locker room incognito, grab her stuff and slip out. Hopefully, Jerry was in the locker room showering. The thought of him naked sent her heart racing again.

The guy at the desk recognized her and let her in even though she didn't have her ID. She would grab her stuff out of the locker room and get out of the place as fast as she could. Her face was hidden behind the locker door when a trio of women came in.

"Man, that dude is perfection."

Katherine peeked through the crack in the locker. The woman Jerry had been spotting had come in with a couple of other women she didn't recognize. The one that had spoken had her hair in a pony-tail so tight, it pulled her eyes into a permanent squint. The third woman sported a purple crew-cut. They all had the same professional builder look-- squared shoulders, muscular, fake tans, and tight bodies.

Katherine was most interested in the one Jerry had been spotting...*and kissing*. And she was pretty, her long hair swung like she was in some sort of princess fairy tale. She wondered if Jerry had already done her.

"I know, right? He's the freshest meat to walk into this gym all year," she said.

The women paused in the little area near her locker. Kat pretended to not notice them as she faked organizing things inside. She wasn't sure if they had seen her or not, but even if they had, it's not like any of them would recognize her.

"That was some kiss you landed on him, Mia," Crew-cut girl said. "Wasn't that coming on a little strong? I don't think you could have gotten a hair between your bodies."

"Maybe. But, I can tell you, he has got one sweet package between his legs."

"You mean he was hard when you hugged him?"

"Like a rock. A loooooooong, wiiiiiiiiide rock." She drew the words long and wide out for emphasis.

Katherine knew exactly what Jerry felt like. She clamped her legs together to fend off the sudden yearning she had for him and concentrated on their conversation.

"Of course he was," Ponytail said. "Any male is going to have a raging hard on when a woman presses against him like that."

"Straight young guys, anyway," Crew-cut said. "My husband once told me that he could fuck anything if it was moving. So, it doesn't take much. Add in a bod like yours pressing into him like that, no question."

Katherine looked down at her much softer, heavier form. The other woman's body was lean, firm and tight. Katherine was in good shape, but she was no body-builder. She had soft, rounded hips. Way bigger boobs. The other woman's had almost disappeared into her chest and pecs. If Jerry was into that boyish look, there was no way he'd be into her. Crew-cut's words, crude as they were, rang true. Men could pretty much get excited over anything. It didn't feel much like a compliment at any rate.

"Yeah. Well, I'm planning on getting that man into the sack," Mia said. "I can guarantee you he's an awesome fuck."

"Good luck with that. He's too pretty for my taste," said Ponytail.

They passed Katherine without looking her direction and went on to the other locker bay. She slung her gym bag over her shoulder and escaped the locker room. She rounded the corner into the lobby and came face to face with Jerry. He looked past her briefly toward the locker room, confusion rippling across his features.

"Mia is just getting into the shower. It'll be a while yet," she said brushing past him.

He grabbed her shoulder. "Whoa, Katherine. Wait. Where are you going?"

She stopped in her tracks and looked down at his hand until he let it drop. "Apparently you are with someone. I am going home."

"Don't go. Not yet."

She stood facing him, her feet in fighting stands and her hands on her. "Why should I stay?"

"What you saw. In the weight room?"

"You and Mia in a full body clench with *wonder woman*?"

He winced. "Yeah that."

"What about it?"

"It's not what it looked like." He looked around the lobby uncomfortably. "Let's go over here. We can have some privacy." He led her around the corner into the hallway behind reception.

"She surprised me with that. I thought she was going to give me a quick hug or peck on the cheek, but the full-body thing...it just happened so fast." He held is hands out. "Honestly. I have no interest in her."

"Your erection said otherwise."

Jerry's head whipped back and his eyes opened and shut a few times. He looked offended. "She was talking about my erection? In the locker room?"

"She described it accurately enough. As well as her plans to fuck you senseless."

His lip curled up in distaste. "Okay, so yeah. I admit...a woman presses her body against me like that, and my dick has a mind of its own. But, just because *it was* doesn't mean *I was*."

His eyes met hers and she looked away, afraid of the intensity she saw there.

He moved in close, gently brushing a stray hair away from her cheek. His fingers skittered down her neck, shoulders, and grasped her hand. "I haven't been able to think about anyone but you since Friday night. Don't you get that? What happened with Mia was her own thing."

She didn't resist when he leaned in and kissed her neck.

Katherine reached out with her right hand and

found the outline of his cock as it strained against his jeans. Even though he had just showered, she could smell his underlying scent. He leaned his forehead against hers in Tango position. He closed his eyes and moaned, his voice deep and low, as she stroked him through the cloth.

"Is this me making you hard? Or is it your dick speaking for itself?"

"You. Katherine, it's all you." He kissed her on her lips, his tongue hungrily found hers.

She palmed his cock and squeezed along the outline. He groaned and broke the kiss. He cupped her cheek with his hand, caressed her lips with his thumb. She sucked it into her mouth, pretending like it was a small cock. She swirled her tongue around the tip. She slid her teeth along the length of his thumb as she released it from her mouth.

"Come home with me, Katherine." His voice was a low growl. It wasn't a request so much as a command.

"Tempting." Her entire body was alive, tingling with anticipation and desire. But, she couldn't go home with him. Her mom was at home. She had the hearing in the morning. *Fuck.* Most importantly, she'd probably end up doing more than she intended. Every ounce of her being wanted him. "I can't tonight."

He wrapped his arms tightly around her, pulling

her in close so his cock was against her stomach. "When?"

"Tomorrow night. I have to get good sleep tonight."

"I can make sure you sleep well." His smile was full of promises she was certain he could keep.

She swayed against him. He shifted and pressed his thigh between her legs. She settled down onto him, sure she'd soak through her workout pants and onto his jeans. She enjoyed the pressure, but it wasn't doing anything for her resolve to say no. She stepped back, breathing in to gain strength.

"Tomorrow," she said. "I really need to get home tonight. My mom's in town, and I have this important work thing."

He tucked a stray curl behind her ear and pulled her close. His eyes twinkled with amusement, or, maybe it was relief, and he grinned. "Tomorrow. I will *definitely* see you tomorrow."

Chapter 14

Katherine spent the entire train ride home wondering why she had said 'no' to Jerry. She *could* have gone to wherever he was staying and spent the night. She would have had time in the morning to rush home, change, and get back to the hearing on time. She could have told him her special suit for the hearing the next day was at home. It sounded like a lame excuse by any standard, but it was the truth. *Part* of the truth, anyway. There was no way she was doing a walk of shame into work on the day of her hearing.

The greater part of it was something Kat didn't really want to think about, but had forced its way into her head anyway. She was fucked up. Who spent ten years doing everything they could to avoid 'regular sex' has all her friends called it? What was so wrong with her that she went to such extraordinary lengths to avoid penetration? She had loved it back in the day. Until the big scare, anyway.

A message chime had her checking for something new from Jerry when she discovered twelve messages on her phone she hadn't noticed. They were all from siblings. She sorted them in her head before reading them. Youngest to oldest. That's how you tend to children's needs. Youngest and most vulnerable first. Katherine read through the texts and responded to each one, finishing just as her train arrived at her stop. Her poor babies. Except, they weren't hers. They were her mother's. In many ways, nothing had changed since she left for DC. It was up to her to keep the family together.

She'd not gotten a straight answer from her mom, she refused to tell anyone what was going on. Dad was being stubborn and not reaching out to Mom. *Mom.* They were acting like teenagers. In spite of all the back and forth with her siblings, Katherine still didn't know what this fight was about. Margaret had suggested her dad had a mistress. Dad? There was no way. He might be charming and flirty, but no. There was no way he'd do that to Mom. One thing she knew was that their dad loved their mom. Worshiped the ground she walked on.

She rushed into the apartment, telling her mom

she'd hit the shower quickly before dinner. Her body was a pent-up ball of exploding energy. She was still amped up from seeing Jerry, and frustrated that she wanted him, but didn't allow herself to be with him.

Katherine let the steamy water wash over her as the realization that her mother had truly fucked her life up hit her full force. People blamed their mothers for a lot of things, but this was real. Who left their ten-year-old to watch four younger kids while they went and did whatever? Up until college, Katherine had been totally in charge of at least one other child.

And yet, she loved her mother with a fierceness she didn't understand. And she loved every single one of her brothers and sisters. It was clear to her why she didn't want her own kids—she already had nine.

She was angry, too. She was pissed that her over-burdened childhood had morphed into a neurosis around sex. If she hadn't already done so much mothering, she wouldn't be so freaked out about getting pregnant.

She tossed on her most comforting pajamas and steeled herself to confront her mom about it all. She needed to know why her mom had needed to have so many babies if she was going to abdicate her responsibilities to her oldest. If she'd only had one or two, maybe Katherine would want to have her own. Maybe her own childhood wouldn't have been so dang filled with kids to detract from her own needs.

There was way too much going on in her head. Her deep lust for Jerry, her anger at her mom, and concern for her siblings all vied with angst over work stuff. She breathed in deeply and tried to focus on one thing at a time. The hearings were only scheduled to last a couple of days, so that would be over soon. Jerry was in town, likely to stay, so maybe there was plenty of time to explore whatever was happening there. The most pressing thing was her mom. She needed to focus on helping her mom get back home.

Her mom was in the kitchen. Cooking. Cleaning. It only lasted in short spurts, like she was trying to make up for it, but didn't know how. The dining room table was already set and in her spot, a plate of food. In spite of her lack of appetite, Katherine found the plate of Salisbury steak with mushroom gravy over mashed potatoes and the huge pile of asparagus, comforting.

If she looked in the fridge, she would probably find mounds of produce, trays of meat, and other makings for her other favorite meals. It was one way that her mom made up for showing up unannounced.

"Katherine. Dear. I can tell something is bugging you. You're awfully quiet."

"I've just got a lot going on at work right now,

Mom. I can't really tend to whatever is going on with you and Dad. It's distracting."

Why couldn't she just confront her mother?

Her mom fiddled with her wine glass, spinning the stem between her fingers. The dark red swirled around the sides of the glass. Katherine had watched her do that many times in the past as she worked out just what to say.

"I'm sorry if my being here is a burden for you. Maybe I should have gone to Margaret's. Or Michael's."

Katherine sighed to interrupt her before she listed all the kids off, a weird sort of countdown from oldest to youngest to induce guilt. "They've all been texting me today, wondering what's going on. The word mistress has been bandied about. Is that right?"

Her mother's eyes widened in surprise, and she waved a dismissive hand at her. "Dalliance, maybe. Mistress? No. It's not like he's set someone up in a secret love nest somewhere."

Katherine took a long swig of wine, upending the glass to empty it and then stared at her mother as the meaning of the words caught up with her. "Wait. Dalliance? What are you saying?"

Her mom regarded Katherine with the patience a kindergarten teacher might give a child who simply doesn't understand something. It drove her nuts, she wasn't some child. How dare she treat her that way?

"Katherine. Your father always comes back to me. I'm the one he loves. The one he cherishes. These...other women. They're just about the sex."

Katherine's fingers tightened around her glass, but she was frozen in position. "Wait. Mom? Women? Are you saying Daddy has done this before? Gone off with...with other women?"

"Well. Actually." She looked up toward the ceiling as if there might be answers there. "It's not always a woman that drives me away. Sometimes he gets all involved with some thing or other. A project."

"Mom...Being involved in some project is way different than being involved with ...."

"Remember the car? He helped Peter with that car. For months. All he could think about was that damn thing. He lived, drank, and breathed that Mustang. Mustang this. Mustang that. Drove me nuts."

Her younger brother had been similarly obsessed with rebuilding the car, enough that the topic had been banned from the conversation table at Christmas. And, now that Kat thought about it, her mom had done one of these mini-vacations away from home that year, too. Actually, her mom had a long history of going off on her own for a week or two as long as Kat could remember--even when she was younger. And she'd left Katherine in charge of everything while she was off.

There were too many issues crashing around in her head. Where had her mother gone off to when Kat was younger? Where had she been when Katherine was home worrying about the kids, feeding them, changing their diapers?

"A car is not the same thing as him cheating on you."

Her mother looked taken aback. "Cheating? Who said anything about cheating on me?"

Katherine leaned forward, her arms on the table, the only thing anchoring her to a suddenly crazy world. "He was with another woman? Kind of the definition of cheating."

"Cheating would imply he goes behind my back, dear. Your father would never lie to me."

Katherine planted her face on the table between her arms. The cool wood was refreshing against her forehead. " Are you saying Daddy isn't having an affair?"

"I wouldn't call it that. No. There are so many lonely women in the neighborhood. He's always been kind-hearted. He was just having sex with Lois Carmichael, to help her feel less alone. You remember her?"

Katherine lifted her head until her chin was on the

table and she could get a good look at her mom. Were they actually having this conversation? "Wait. What? Mom, he's having an affair with Mrs. Carmichael? Bucky's mom?"

Her mom broke into a big grin. "That's right. You and Bucky were quite the thing in high school, weren't you?"

Mrs. Carmichael had been the mom everyone on the street had been afraid of. Puritanical and maniacal when it came to just about anything. Bucky had rebelled against his mom hard, and they had broken up because he was just too wild for her. Katherine took a big gulp of her wine.

"But no, that's what I'm trying to tell you. He's not having an affair. He's just having sex with her."

"Why in the world would Dad be..." she couldn't even finish the sentence. Mrs. Carmichael was older than her parents, and her husband had been ancient even in high school. He'd died what, five years ago? Ten? Kat couldn't remember. The image of her dad with Bucky's mom was just too disturbing. She always thought of herself as an adult when it came to talking about sex. But, when the conversation centered around her parent's sex life, she shuddered. "Oh, jeez, Mom?"

"Well, his decision and choices in these things are something I have agreed to not dwell on. The rule is, as long as he's saving enough of himself for me, and is attentive to my needs, I don't put any rules on his extra-curricular activities."

Katherine couldn't think of any sort of appropriate response.

"Of, for heaven's sake, Katherine, pull your chin off the table. You look ridiculous. You can't possibly pretend you didn't know we have an open marriage."

"You certainly didn't announce it when I was ten. Come on Mom. You guys hid it when we were kids."

"True. But well, it was no secret."

"Am I hallucinating? Mom, are you telling me that you and dad...wait." A sudden and horrifying thought filled her with dread. "Are you saying you both slept around? The whole time you were married?"

"Of course not."

A strange sense of relief flooded through her.

"Mom, that's what an open marriage is. When the people who are married have sex with other people."

"Or not. Believe me, I know what an open marriage is, Katherine, and it's the only way I would have survived living with that man for thirty years. Your father is, well, best put, hypersexual." She reached out and grabbed one of Katherine's hands. "As much as I enjoy sex, I can only do it so many times in a day."

Kat jumped up, unable to take any more, her hands shooting into the air in the universal signal of surrender. "Stop. Mom, just stop. I don't think I can take any more of this." She reached for the bottle of wine and emptied the dregs into her glass.

Her mom sighed heavily, her lips drawn tightly together in disapproval. "Well, my point is, dear. I'm not angry at your father because he was sleeping around. I'm angry because he is spending too much time with her."

It was then that everything became crystal clear to her. Katherine desperately wanted to shove her fingers in her ears and sing a song to cover up anything her mom might say next. The part of her that relished horror films and couldn't turn her face away from the screen knowing someone was about to get splattered won out. But she wasn't about to stay quiet anymore, she had something to say to her mom. She wasn't a compliant, complacent kid anymore, she was a grown woman and her mom had questions to answer.

Chapter 15

Childhood memories flittered through her mind like an old-fashioned movie--the nights her father disappeared, the times her mother was gone and left her in charge. These snippets of meaningless scenes now formed a wholly different narrative. She'd spent most of her life filtering out the bits of her life that didn't make sense.

The strange jokes and innuendos she had heard all her life—from her parents, from her aunts and uncles, from the neighbors, and even her siblings. She realized then, that they all knew. And, just like not seeing Ashley's visits to Caroline as anything, she'd chosen not to see the goings on in her own house as she grew up.

Her mother had just said it. *You can't pretend you didn't know. It was no secret.*

Ashley's words from the other night echoed in her head. *After all those times you saw me leaving Caroline Crawford's room.*

It was no secret.

As she scoured her memories, the proof of it was all there. She'd never had a conversation with her brothers or sisters about it, but their oddly cryptic jokes suddenly made sense. And all that time, when she'd stayed home to feed and fuss over the kids, her mom was what, out having sex with someone besides her dad? Or off in a pout because he wasn't being attentive enough to her?

"So you left me to take care of the kids while you and Dad went around and screwed other people?"

Her mother started. "Katherine? What?"

"I'm the one who had to take care of Margaret and Michael. I'm the one who did the dishes every day. I did it so much, I don't want kids. I don't want to be married. Do you have any idea how fucked up I am?"

It was her mother's turn to look surprised. "You are not."

"Mom, did you know I haven't had intercourse with a man since I was nineteen?"

"Oh, no, sweetie. You've had lots of boyfriends. Certainly, at thirty, you've slept with them."

She threw her hands up in exasperation. "Did you hear what I said? I said I haven't had intercourse. I had a pregnancy scare when I was nineteen and decided sex just wasn't worth the worry it caused. I didn't want to take care of a kid, I felt like I'd already been a mom."

"But you weren't actually pregnant, were you?"

"No mom, I wasn't. But I didn't tell you because I didn't want you to worry. Just like I didn't tell you about Michael's shooting the BB gun at Joan, Margaret passing out on drugs and booze when she was fifteen, or Joan asking me to take her for birth control pills. We all kept things from you so you don't go away. I took care of the family."

Her mom sat back, hands wringing together on her lap. "I did what I had to do to stay sane."

"Because you had too many of us."

"Maybe. But, can you imagine the world without any of you?"

Katherine opened a second bottle of wine. "I can't. But your having so many children was a decision you made that completely messed up my life. Don't you see that? Whenever you went away, who do you think was there for everyone else? Dad?"

Her mother looked away, eyes lowered. "I'm so sorry Katherine. I hadn't realized what a burden I had placed on your shoulders. You were always so grown up, I thought you would be okay."

Kat poured them each some more wine. *What did it mean to be okay?*

"But, really dear, I think you remember things a little different than reality. Sure, you had some responsibilities, but there was always an adult around. Someone to be in charge. Not you."

Kat wasn't sure who was better at revising her history—her or her mother. "Did you even ask if you could come this week? You just showed up."

"How have you gotten along all this time without sex? Is that why you haven't settled down?"

Kat closed her eyes and spread her fingers out wide, pressing them into the table. She wasn't going to go into this again. She'd left Jerry at the gym, but maybe she should have gone with him. She'd probably be naked and on her third orgasm by now if she had.

"Mom, I love you. But, I want you to go home tomorrow."

"You are not fucked up, Katherine. You need to hear this. So, maybe you have some unusual notions when it comes to sex, but it's kept you safe. And I bet you've not had any unwanted pregnancies or diseases either."

"That's not the point, Mom."

"You had a good education, went to college, and now you work for a man who is likely going to be president one day. I personally think you've done fine."

"Mom, I'm going to bed."

"You're hearing is tomorrow? Can I come?"

"Yeah. Mom, you can come." She sighed. "Be up early so we can leave at 7:30." What use was it to argue? Her mom would stay as long as she was planning on staying. She left her mom to clean up after dinner and closed herself up in her bedroom.

She climbed into bed and tossed and turned for a long time. She just couldn't drown out the conversation she had just had with her mom. Everything had changed. She had no idea how their relationship would move forward from here. Or how she would ever look at her dad without imagining him with Mrs. Carmichael.

She checked her phone when it was clear she wasn't going to fall asleep straight away.

There was a text from Jerry that she'd missed while she was in the shower.

It was a simple emoji heart.

Chapter 16

Katherine introduced her mom to people in the office, though she knew Carleen already. Carleen had worked at her father's law firm for years before becoming Congressman Pierce's personal assistant, and her boss. Her Dad didn't have great things to say about Congressman Pierce. He had 'stolen' Carleen from the firm when he left, but it had worked out well for Katherine in the long run.

The hearing was scheduled to start at 9:00 in the Cannon Caucus Room. The room was set up like any hearing, but the number of chairs was drastically reduced compared to some of the more famous proceedings. This kind of hearing was important to the people involved, but there would be no news cameras covering it. There might be a reporter or two, but that would be it.

Her mom took the room in with a full three hundred sixty degree turn, examining it from ceiling to floor. "Television doesn't do it justice. It's beautiful. Just as grand as anything you'd see at Versailles."

"Maybe not as much gold, but yeah. It's pretty cool." Katherine said. The last time she'd been in here it was with about thirty other people in yoga pants doing impossible positions. Once you've done downward dog in a room, it doesn't retain the same majesty as it might otherwise. She wouldn't ruin the experience for her mom by mentioning it. "It's quite versatile. People rent it out for various functions all the time."

Her mom settled down in a chair in the back as Katherine and the rest of her team organized themselves at a front table. For a moment, she worried about her mom. That she would get bored, or that she needed to take care of her. Her mom was a big girl; she'd be fine.

People trickled into the room. Kat ignored what was happening behind her as she arranged her folders exactly as she needed them. When everyone was assembled, she was so focused on the proceedings she didn't even think to look around.

Katherine's job was pretty simple. Keep facts and

figures organized and ready to hand over to lead counsel as he needed it. As the hearing was called to order, Carleen handed Kat the completed background checks on the new witnesses they'd only found out about on Monday. It reminded her she hadn't heard back from Kenny about Jerry. She wondered if he'd found anything of interest.

"CGF has a good rep, and the guys they have testifying have good bona fides."

Katherine flipped open the background file anyway.

Marcus Griffin was thirty-two, six foot six inches tall, played pro-basketball for the Boston Celtics for three years and returned to school to get his Ph.D. from MIT. He was married, had two kids, went to the local Baptist church and volunteered as a scout leader. She studied his photo. He reminded her of a younger Denzel Washington.

Grant Tanner looked familiar to her. She couldn't place him, though. Her memory for faces wasn't nearly as good as her memory for words. Another stand-up guy with degrees from Cal Tec and RPI. Divorced with two kids. He had spent a couple years working for Shell Oil, but was fired for whistle blowing. Now that was interesting. What was Walker doing bringing in people who typically served against his better interest?

Gerard Porter. She stared at the picture, goose-bumps breaking out all over her skin. She flipped back to Grant's photo to place him squarely in New York. She flipped back to Gerard Porter. But not Gerard. No. He'd called himself Jerry.

Gerard. Jerry. Gerry? Had she misheard him? She'd been thinking of him as Jerry for nearly five days now. Her jaw dropped open as the realization that this guy she'd been day-dreaming over--the guy who had asked her if she believed in love at first sight, the guy who had danced her into oblivion, the guy who had promised to see her today--was very likely sitting behind her, waiting for his turn to testify.

She replayed the moment he'd said his name in the bar. He had said, "I'm Jerry."

That's what she had *heard*, anyway.

She replayed the conversation in her head.

I'm Katherine.

I'm Jerry.

Jerry?

Close enough.

He'd winced a little. Was it because she'd mispro-nounced his name? Had he actually said Gerard, and she heard Jerry? It had been one of the more mellow bars, but it had still been crowded with people. Plus, she'd had a couple of martinis by then. Whatever. It didn't really matter. The misconception was there.

It only mattered that he was here. Behind her.

Suddenly, she was sure he was watching her. She could feel his eyes on the back of her head.

I'll definitely see you tomorrow.

And he knew who she was. How long had he known who she was? And he didn't say anything about it last night at the gym. She almost went home with him. Thank God her good sense kept her from it.

She waited until someone new was called to speak, using the excuse to swivel in her seat, pretending to be scanning the crowd as a whole. He was there. In the second row from the front. In a classic black suit with a stunning silk tie.

He was staring directly at her, as if he'd been sitting there this whole time waiting for her to turn around. He sat with his legs crossed, hands lightly clasped over his knee. The corner of his mouth quirked upward in amusement. Not a hint of surprise.

Had he known all along who she was? Had he and his buddies shown up at that bar somehow knowing she would be there? That was impossible. That *had* to be a coincidence.

She ran through all their conversations from the weekend. She'd dissed lobbyists. He had said he was a scientist.

They hadn't talked at all about work. He'd asked her once what she did for a living, and she had intentionally been nebulous. *I work on the hill as a staffer.* She'd been intentionally vague about what she did.

She looked at the file again. He had only told her that he was a scientist. He was a scientist who worked for a think-tank that was known for its objectivity and even-handedness--a rare commodity indeed. As a scientist, he would have to be on the right side of this debate. At least he wasn't here to destroy this legislation.

There wouldn't be any conflict of interest there. Unless of course, his working for CGF and their hanging out together could be seen as some sort of collusion on Congressman Pierce's part to persuade the scientist to alter his testimony. Lincoln had no way of knowing where she was on the weekend. Sure, he knew she'd be in New York, but even she had no idea what bars she would be going to.

Had he been a plant in New York, sent there to hang out with her to cause a fake scandal? They did go to the same place to start out their weekend almost every month. It was cozy and talkable. And she had been tagged there on Instagram almost every month for the last year or two. So it was possible to find a trend. But that...was ludicrous. Stupid. Paranoid.

Kenny would say there is no such thing as coincidence, but the two of them ending up in the same bar on Friday night was totally bizarre. She wanted to text

Kenny and get his opinion, but texting would be disrespectful of the hearings. Carleen and every Congressman on the panel would give her the death stare. She didn't dare.

Her hands shook as she put the file down.

Carleen leaned in, dropping her voice to a whisper. "What is going on with you?"

Kat tightened her smile and did what her mom would have told her to do. Buck up. "It's just...this guy?" She tapped the photo of Gerard. "I met him in NY on the weekend. We danced for hours. We almost had sex."

Carleen's eyes closed for a second as she considered this. "That is quite a coincidence."

"I know, right? Could someone have set us up to make it look bad? Who wouldn't want this deal to go through?"

"If we were colluding with CGF to ensure their testimony was in our favor, you can bet Senator Watkins would be all over that."

"Why? Destroying this deal wouldn't do anything for his people."

Carleen's eyebrows furrowed together. "You think Senator Watkins cares about his constituents? This deal is against his pocketbook, but he can't come out and say that he'd be out millions personally when so many people would benefit from it."

"Damn. We didn't talk about work. He didn't ask me..." Katherine paused. But he did. He asked her a couple times what it was she did for a living, but that was something everyone asked all the time. "Well, he didn't push me about my job, and he just said he was a scientist and was moving to D.C. soon."

It was all coincidence. It had to be. Katherine tuned out everything but what was happening in front of her then. She refused to let her personal drama leak into her professional life any more than it already had. It took all her will-power to not turn around and look at Jerry. Gerard.

AN EXCRUCIATING TWO HOURS LATER, her mom texted to tell her she needed to go outside for a walk. She'd find her own way back to the apartment. Without thinking, Katherine swiveled in her chair again and saw that, indeed, her mom was gone.

She swept her eyes over Jerry. She kept her expression free from showing emotion, she wanted him to see only her poker face.

Gerard. Whoever.

He met her eyes, but he was no longer smiling.

Chapter 17

As the hearing broke for lunch, Katherine organized her files, taking her time hoping that the entire room had cleared out behind her.

No such luck. Gerard stood near the only door that was open, effectively making it impossible for her to leave without passing within inches of him.

Kathleen handed her stack of binders over to Cheyenne "Take these to my office, please?"

Cheyenne nodded silently and followed Carleen out of the room, her arms laden with paperwork.

Kat started towards the doorway. Her fate was inevitable; she might as well meet it head on.

"Well, well, well...look what we have here," he said.

Kat shook her head, and took Gerard by the elbow. The hallways just outside the caucus room were lined with congressional offices and were remarkable for their sound-carrying properties. Whispers in the halls could be heard from amazing lengths away, so she guided Gerard out of the hearing room, down a flight of steps and into an abandoned hallway. It was actually part of the building that was under renovation, but not currently being worked on.

"Why didn't you correct me when I called you Jerry?" she asked.

"I said Gerard the other night, but when you got it wrong I thought it would be impolite to correct you."

"And when were you planning to tell me?"

They faced each other in mirrored positions, hands on hips feet separated into a basic fighting stance. Had they really Tangoed only four days ago? She could still feel the heat of his breath on her neck.

"I almost did last night, but then I thought it would be more interesting if I showed up today. I wasn't entirely sure you didn't know who I was until you turned around earlier. I could see you were surprised."

"Why didn't you tell me you were a lobbyist for CGF?"

"I'm a scientist."

"Once you get money for trying to sway an opinion, you are a lobbyist. You didn't tell me you were a lobbyist."

"You had just dissed the entirety of two professions. I didn't know you. You think I would cop to being either?"

"And you've known who I am since when?"

"I googled you Sunday afternoon."

"Sunday?" So he hadn't known who she was before they met. Before they danced. Maybe Friday and Saturday night had been real. "Are you sure it was Sunday?"

"Want me to show you my browser history? You have your phone info set to public, so, when your text came through, it gave me your whole name. So I knew your name, but nothing else."

So it had been just a coincidence that they both showed up at the same club Friday night.

"I was getting ready to text you Sunday night, just to check in. But I decided to google you first. See if I could think of something clever to say if I knew you a little better."

She'd been known to do the same thing. Hell, Kenny was going to do a full security check on him, but she didn't have his last name, so she was still waiting on the info.

He ran a hand through his hair and sighed. "I googled your name with DC and it came up with tons of hints. Including a pretty revealing photo of you and Lincoln Pierce."

"You're jealous of a photo on the internet, of me

and my boss?"

"You know the photo?"

Katherine could guess which one. There had been an over-eager paparazzi reporter who had snapped a photo of the two of them at a fundraising banquet shortly after Katherine had started working for the Congressman.

"I was brand new in DC. I chose the wrong dress for the occasion. The reporter got a great angle of my cleavage and the Senator's arms around my shoulders. Throw in a racy headline and there you have it. But there was no inappropriate liaison. End of story."

Fortunately, Link's absolutely rigid rule about keeping the door open was well known and the reporter had gone back to Indiana with his tail between his legs.

"You knew who I was at the gym last night. You didn't mention that you were testifying today, or that you knew who I was. You let me continue to call you Jerry."

He moved a little closer to her and she stepped back, running into the wall behind her.

"Frankly, last night, I was more worried about what was going on with Mia. I could see you were upset when you saw her kissing me. By the time we were hot and heavy in the hallway, I was thinking you'd come back to my room with me. I wanted to tell you. Explain everything. I figured it would be awkward. And, see? I was right."

"So you found out who I was on Sunday and left me hanging for two days. All you had to do was text me about your concerns."

He placed his hands on either side of her head. "I wanted to see you face to face. Texting usually mucks things up for me." He placed his forehead against hers. "I'm sorry. I meant to reach out, but it was awkward-- me knowing all this stuff about you. It was uneven and too much to explain on a text."

She searched his eyes and found only honesty. And mutual longing.

"Look, there's no conflict of interest if we openly date each other. We just can't talk about your testimony. Besides, you're going to be done testifying later today anyway. Poof, no problem, right?" His proximity was intoxicating. She tilted her head up. He gave her a gentle Eskimo Kiss, tapping her nose gently against his.

"If people see us together, won't they think we're working on some sort of deal? I am, officially, a lobbyist."

"If we couldn't date lobbyists, no one working on the hill would ever go out."

"I'm sorry." He kissed her gently on the lips. "Let me make it up to you."

Katherine wasn't sure what to make of him. He

hadn't said anything when she'd dissed lobbyists and lawyers when they met. He hadn't corrected her butchering his name. Gerard was so much sexier than Jerry.

Hey. He's a lobbyist.

If she could get him to the Washington Monument, he'd be her fourth dot on her bingo card. She could go out with him tonight and the CIA dude as scheduled the following evening and win the game. The only problem was, she had no desire to go out with the CIA guy.

She flushed as she realized she was even contemplating kissing another man after she'd been so upset about Gerard kissing another woman. She felt a little ridiculous for having been so upset about Gerard kissing Mia in the gym.

The buoyant feeling of hopeful attraction to Gerard flared to life. Things were going to be just fine. At least for a while. Until he tired of her rules...rules he didn't even know about yet. She kept getting so far ahead of herself at times.

"Let's meet up at the end of the day and go from there, shall we?" He slid his hands down her body before pulling her in close and kissing he deeply. He rested his forehead against hers again, bringing the magic of their Tango back to life.

She could barely speak. "It's a date."

Chapter 18

When Gerard texted to set up the logistics of the date, she chose a restaurant that was a five-minute walk from the Washington Monument. If she was going to have a date with a lobbyist, she was not going to miss out on scoring one for the game. One of the rules of the BINGO game was that they couldn't tell any of the guys they were playing. Part of the fun was getting the men to agree to go to local tourist attractions as part of a date. She didn't think it would be hard to entice Gerard into going for a walk after dinner. How was it that Gerard, especially with a little French lilt to it, was so much sexier than Jerry? She must have been a bit more drunk Friday night than she had thought to mishear that.

The restaurant was an upscale Oaxacan restaurant. Decor and prices were unlike anything she'd ever run into on her two trips to Oaxaca. The food, on the other hand, was totally authentic. The waiter put down a bowl of hot chapulines and two glasses of mezcal in front of them as they sat down. She smiled mischievously. One of her goals in life was to travel everywhere. Having a man who was as adventurous as she was when it came to food was important to her.

Gerard examinee them, a dubious expression on his face. "What are these?"

She tossed a handful into her mouth. The chile and lime complemented the sweet crispy bits. She chased the food down with a sip of mezcal. The combination in her mouth was a happy party. She looked at him without saying anything. "They are delicious. Try them."

"These are some sort of bug, aren't they?" He grimaced before popping a small handful into his mouth. As he chewed, his expression shifted from one of complete skepticism, to thoughtful, to surprised. He chased his down with the mezcal and nodded. "Okay. I think I just ate a bunch of..." his eyes narrowed on the bowl again. "Crickets. I just ate a handful of tiny baby crickets. Deep fried baby crickets."

"You're not vegan are you?" she asked.

He looked down at himself, puffing up his chest a little bit. "Do I look vegan to you?"

She considered him seriously for a minute. No. He most certainly did not. "I've known some buff guys who ate vegan. It's a healthy diet."

Gerard shrugged and downed a larger serving. "I would never have ordered them, but I like them."

He had passed one of her tests. She liked a man who would take chances, a man who could be comfortable in uncomfortable situations. Anyone who would willingly eat crickets definitely got a positive score in the food department.

As they relaxed into their meal, Katherine found herself telling Gerard about her mom's latest revelation about their open marriage.

"You don't seem comfortable with an arrangement like that," he said.

"No. I'm not. I mean...I always thought I'd find the one guy, the one true love and get married. We'd live happily ever after and spend all our disposable income on fine dining and traveling."

"Sounds like your mom did find her one and only."

"I always thought my dad worshiped her."

"That polyamorous stuff doesn't work for everyone. My mom always said she loved us kids the same but different, so maybe it's like that. Your dad loves your mom, but he has physical needs outside that love."

"That's how my mom put it. I just don't think it would work for me." She looked up at him. Was it the same for him?

"I'm a one girl at a time guy. We have that in common." He reached across the table and took her hand. "I can only dance with one person at a time." He lifted her hand to his lips and kissed her palm.

Little shivers skimmed across her skin. She studied him closely in the restaurant's dimming light, ran a finger along his already familiar jawline. There was a youthfulness about him she hadn't noticed. "How old are you?"

His jaw tightened defensively. "Old enough."

"I'm thirty. How. Old. Are. You?"

"Twenty-four."

She did the math. "But you have a Ph.D." He sure as hell didn't present like a typical twenty-four-year old. She would have sworn he was more her age or even older--there was a maturity about him. Six years wasn't that much of a difference, was it?

"I was something of a child prodigy. I graduated high school at sixteen, college at eighteen, had my Masters at nineteen, and my Ph.D. by twenty-two."

"Wow. That is a fast-track. Did you ever...have time for fun?"

"I've been making up for that the last couple of

years. Living so close to New York has been a lot of fun."

"Given how well you dance, I am guessing all you ever did was study and dance."

His eyes darkened a little bit. She had touched on a raw nerve.

They shifted into typical conversation people have on a first date. The kind you have before you've kissed, before you've gotten off together over the phone, before you talk about liking oral sex.

"What's your full name?"

Kat smiled. "Katherine Agatha Joan O'Malley. My mom wanted to honor both of my grandmothers. But, she thought Agatha and Joan were outdated, so she put them as my middle names."

"Agatha maybe, but not Joan."

"Yeah, well my mom kind of forgot about that when she named my baby sister Joan. I think she actually forgot it was one of my middle names when she was reaching for a name."

Gerard laughed. "If she's anything like my mom, you only get your whole name when she's upset." He screwed up his face and raised his voice to falsetto. "Gerard Frances Porter, get inside right now."

"Oh, you could be an actor," she said.

They discovered more in common with each other than just dancing. They liked the same televisions shows—though neither watched that much television. They both loved Steve Martin to an unreasonable degree, and they both wanted to learn how to scuba dive.

"My sister, Margaret, learned to dive before her honeymoon. The pictures she brought back from Hawaii were amazing."

Gerard held up a hand. "Hey, wait a second. I thought you said your sister's name was Joan."

Katherine took a deep breath. "That's my youngest sister. I don't expect you to get this straight right away, but I have nine siblings. Margaret, Michael, Simon, Jude, David, Gabriel, Mathew, Joan and Justin." She rattled them off with a practiced speed. "I've known my mother to run through all of us just to get to Justin."

"Wow. That's a lot of kids."

"Two sets are twins. Simon and Jude are twenty-seven. Joan and Justin are the babies and the only two left at home. They're juniors in high school this year."

"I envy you so much Katherine. I only have Carl. We both wanted a sister so bad it wasn't funny. We petitioned our parents to have one, but they never granted it. Probably for the best. We were a handful."

"Two boys, try seven boys." Katherine rolled her eyes. "There was so much testosterone in my house, it was sort of contagious. I'm kind of bossy."

"Kind of?"

She threw her napkin at his face. He caught it and he tossed it back to her. "I like bossy women. Confident women who know what they want."

Their eyes met and held for a long time. Another type of conversation passed between them—it was a silent understanding, a simple knowing of the kind that happens between couples from across the room when their eyes meet and they *just know* what the other is thinking.

By the time dessert came, she was feeling like they'd known each for months, not days. They ordered the special for the evening that included a flan, a sweet corn tamale, and a spiced thickened hot chocolate with a churro. It was an odd combination, but the elements together were delicious. They ended up doing a little spoon fight over the last scoop of flan, but he let her win.

They stepped out of the restaurant into the cool spring evening. The air was chilly without being breezy. Katherine took his arm as they strolled along.

"I hope you don't mind walking for a bit. Sitting all day makes me twitchy, and I need to get some movement in."

She felt the tiniest bit of guilt as she turned toward the Washington Monument. If things worked out between them, it would just be the memory of a first date. The worse that could happen was she was falling in love with a man who would end up leaving her like everyone else. At least she was going to be one mark closer to winning the Bingo game. It was like she was hedging a bet, she wasn't willing yet to trust him completely.

Chapter 19

The sun had long since set, but the lights around the monument at night lit the base up so that it shown brightly. There was something majestic in its simplicity. The fact it was incredibly phallic had its own set of connotations in a town filled with men always vying for power. An interesting choice of design by whoever it was who designed it. She held up her phone slightly apologetically. "I like to keep track of the places I'm visiting. Sort of a record."

She took a selfie with the monument behind her.

"Ever been up to the top?" he asked as they got to the edge of the park.

"Nope. When I first moved here it had just been damaged by an earthquake and was closed. It's been fixed for a couple years, though. I should plan on going up sometime."

"It looks bigger from here. I'm used to seeing it from the other end of The Mall."

She led him toward the pathway that would take them directly to the base of the monument. She guessed that she was close enough for it to count, but there was something awkward about just asking him to kiss her right there, in the open expanse of grass with cars whizzing nearby. And, he was genuinely interested in the monument itself.

"Let's walk around it. Now that I'm here I want to see when it's open to visitors."

"Fifty flags. It looks pretty cool with them all flying like that."

There were several signs around the base of the monument explaining it was, once again, closed. This time for another two years to put in an elevator.

"I'd rather climb up the steps than use an elevator."

"That's not very accessible of you," she teased.

"I like climbing. It makes me feel like I've really earned the view when I'm up there. When I visit places, I like to do that. I climbed the Eiffel tower rather than take the elevator up. I even climbed the World Trade Center before it collapsed."

She tilted her head at him, skeptical. "Wouldn't you have been like ten years old on 9/11?"

"Actually I was eight. But, my father worked in the

Trade Center, and we did it as part of a fund raiser the weekend before the attack."

"Oh. Was he..." How did you ask someone if their father died in the attack?

He shook his head. "Oh. No. He was home that day with a bad back from doing the climb."

This conversation was not very kiss-inducing. He was looking about as depressed as she was feeling for bringing it up.

"Well, there's not much to do here at night."

He kissed her. Just like that.

His mouth was warm and sweet from their dessert. After their previous two make-out sessions, she knew what to expect from him. He was less tentative and more demanding this time around; his movements had transformed from furtive to knowing. He was a fast learner.

This time, his hands roamed freely down her back and cupped her bottom to pull her close. She felt the full measure of his erection. She glanced around and was disappointed to see a number of other couples walking around. They couldn't go very far in public. As much as she wanted to drop to her knees right there, she knew she would have to wait.

"For the third time now, will you come with me to my hotel?" he asked.

There was nothing more that she wanted right at

that moment then to explore the man's body with her hands, her mouth, her tongue—to get him naked beneath her. Besides, a night away from her mother was just what she needed. To do that, though, she'd have to explain her personal rules about sex. Even though she had the realization just how messed up her reasoning was, she wasn't ready to just dump ten years' worth of pretty good policy.

Guys reacted one of two ways to her particular requirements for a sleepover. They either called her a crazy cock-tease or they thought it over and decided to have fun her way. Either way, they never stayed with her longer than a few months. It was one of the hardest rules she had ever imposed upon herself, but she was adamant about it. She wasn't ready to budge.

"I can, but I have some rules when it comes to sex you should know about."

His eyes narrowed just a little bit as he looked at her sideways. "Rules? I'm pretty good with rules. Especially when sex is involved. Shoot."

She waited until they were under a light so she could get a decent reading on his response. "I, uhm... don't allow penetration."

He tilted his head and leaned in a little bit. "No penetration of any kind?"

"I suppose you could get all semantic about it, but basically no penis in vagina or ass."

"Mouth? You are okay with giving head, though?" He asked.

"I am more than okay with giving head. It's definitely something I've mastered. I've learned to do all sorts of tricks with my tongue...and jaw." She batted her lashes up at him. "It's not that I'm a prude or anything. And, I want you to have great time."

Gerard swallowed hard. "I think I can work with that."

Usually what happened next was the guy would ask *why* she had the no-fucking rule or ask what they would be doing instead. Most often, guys would freak out about dealing with a thirty-year-old virgin. They often jumped to the conclusion she had made a freakish promise to her dad when she was ten for religious reasons.

Not Gerard though. He was either genuinely fine with her requirements, or he was just trying to get naked; and then she'd get the pouting. But there was no pouting, no pleading, no begging, no promises of condoms, not yet anyway. His gentle and playful acceptance was refreshing.

"So, exactly how have you managed to not have sex for 30 years--or at least fifteen of them? You have to have come up against some guys who pushed back."

"There is so much more to sex than intercourse."

She said the last word with derision, as if it meant nothing to her.

Most of the men she had dated were completely ready for a woman to make a few decisions about "what next" and exactly "how" they would proceed, so it generally worked in her favor. She dated powerful men whose days were filled with decision making, and they liked the respite from having to make the call.

Her rules of engagement rendered some of them clueless. A couple of guys thought that their dicks were the appetizer, main course, and dessert when it came to sex--in the beginning.

Fortunately, men were as pliable as clay when it came to sex. Not that she had been through that many. Maybe five a year? So, thirty or so men had been confronted with her rules and left her bed with dozens of new tricks for their future girlfriends. She'd had the wife of an ex actually come up to her and thank her for doing such a good job training her husband. It was a little awkward.

"Have you actually never been tempted to just throw your rules out the window and actually go all the way?" he asked.

She dropped her eyes to the bulge in his pants. "As a matter of fact. No. I haven't."

Mostly. At least not until the other night.

It was very complicated, and she didn't even get

into the fact she never wanted kids of her own, and the fear of pregnancy was her only reason for this little rule of hers. Her argument had no logic, but even so, she didn't care. She had an IUD in place, she had refused any and all offers, no matter how enticing.

His lips quirked upward and he pulled her into his arms. "What exactly do you propose we do tonight in my hotel room then?"

She grasped his earlobe between her teeth and let it slide out slowly. "Well, I think the first thing we should do is get naked and look at each other for ten minutes straight, no touching."

"With the lights on?"

She turned her head to get a good look at his face to see if he was kidding. It didn't look like he was. She did have six years on him. That was six years' worth of being creative enough in bed with men to keep them satisfied without actually fucking. "Of course. Gerard..."

He kissed the tip of her nose.

"How many women have you slept with?" she asked.

"How many men have you not slept with?"

"Touché. Let me rephrase that. I have learned that the best way to keep to my rules and to have healthy and satisfying sexual relationships, is to speak frankly about sex."

"I like the sound of that. I'll be honest. I've been much more of a doer, and most of the women I've been with haven't been particularly secure in their own bodies. Having you suggest that all I do is look at you for ten minutes straight is hot as hell." He pushed the hair off his forehead. "I haven't slept around all that much, but only two women I've been with were cool with the lights being on. No one else has ever suggested I just stare at her naked body."

He shifted his stance and slid his hand into his pants to adjust himself. "Honestly, just *thinking* about you naked is exciting."

Chapter 20

Katherine was used to being in charge in bed, mostly out of necessity. Tell a guy he can do anything but fuck and all he can think about is fucking.

Her being in charge to start with was mostly necessary because of her rules. It was wearing. Tiring. She longed for a man who came to her with enough creative energy that she wasn't the one who always had to tell them what to do. Until she had a guy who she was sure had been snipped and wasn't interested in children, she was willing to pay that price.

The hotel was convenient to the hill as well as Georgetown. Apparently, Gerard would be spending a good time there as a consultant in one of their science programs. Katherine was still unclear on exactly what it was he did, even though he'd explained it to her over dinner. It was a very esoteric branch of astrophysics that most people wouldn't understand. It turned out that Neil deGrasse Tyson had been a mentor for his Ph.D. thesis project. They were real-life friends.

Gerard's hotel was too far away to walk, so they grabbed a taxi. They made out in the back of the cab like teenagers who knew they'll be caught any minute.

The boutique hotel didn't look like much from the outside, but it had obviously had extensive renovations done since its original construction. Boring square seventies on the outside hid a marble and cherry wood interior remodel.

Gerard pulled her into his arms as they got into his room. But, it wasn't just a room. It was a suite and set up for a long-term stay. The door opened onto a small living room, kitchen and dining table in the first half of the room, and the king bed with bathroom in the other half. A sliding door separated the two rooms.

The furnishings were new, and she was pretty sure she could still smell the fresh paint on the walls. It was highly-decorated for a modern male guest. All grey furnishings, metal and glass side tables, black and red accent throw pillows.

"Oh, I see," she said. "They really want you to stay here until you find someplace to live."

"Yeah. Full kitchen. In room laundry. It's an upscale apartment with room and maid service." He pointed to the phone. "Should I order up a bottle of champagne?"

The Mezcal and the wine she'd had at dinner had been enough for her. "No, thanks."

Katherine did not want to waste time. She had been thinking about him way too long and too many times to let him get out of her grasp now. She took his hand and headed straight into the bedroom.

"Sit down. Me first."

He perched on the edge of the bed, hands on his knees, his full attention on her.

She faced him and unbuttoned her blouse, letting it fall open, then turned from him. She looked over her shoulder at him as she let the blouse shimmy off her arms and down to her fingertips. She caught it and tossed it over to the chair next to the bed. She unzipped her skirt and peeled it off her hips, down her thighs, and past her legs, bending over so that he got an eyeful of her round ass, covered in lacy underwear.

She stood up and faced him in just her bra and panties. He was watching every move she made. She'd done similar strips for other men, but it had never felt so raw before. As a matter of fact, she felt like she was getting naked in front of a man for the first time. She paused and met his eyes.

"You like what you see so far?" she asked.

He nodded, but didn't say anything. Just narrowed his vision to a spot on her knee.

"I fell off my bike when I was ten. Really bad road rash."

She reached behind her and unclasped her bra. She let it fall off her arms and down to the floor. Her breasts were large, but buoyant, young and firm. They swayed gently at the freedom. She cupped them in her palms and swirled her thumbs around her nipples until they were hard little nubs.

Kat reached a finger between the elastic band around the top of her panties and her skin. She pulled at it, teasing. She turned away from him again before bending over and pulling the panties free, giving him a very clear view of her very wet slit.

She stood up slowly and looked over her shoulder to meet Gerard's eyes. He shifted in his seat but remained where he was. She turned to face him one more time, letting him see her naked from head to toe.

It took all her effort to not hold her hands to cover herself as he examined her. She wasn't used to caring what others might think, and she had a sudden desire to know that Gerard liked what he saw. She wanted him to want her, but she felt exposed in a way she'd never felt before.

"Pretty standard equipment," she said.

Gerard's mouth had gone slack, and he snapped it

shut as if he were coming out of some sort of trance. "Right."

She leaned over him, hands on his knees and kissed him on the lips. Gently. Almost chaste. "Your turn." She brushed her breasts against his face. Sliding her hands down his arms to his hands, she pulled him up off the bed.

She ripped off the covers. Sheets just get in the way. She plumped up two pillows and made herself comfortable facing him with her legs crossed comfortably at the ankles.

He swallowed hard before ripping off his clothes. He may have torn a button off in his haste to get naked, and his clothes billowed like little parachutes as they floated to the floor in ragged heaps. He stood there, naked and fully erect in front of her in about five seconds, hands out to his side, palms up.

"No slow striptease?"

He looked at his strewn clothing. "You want me to put them back on and start over?"

She suppressed a laugh. "No." She patted the spot next to her on the bed.

Gerard launched himself onto the bed and she bounced toward him. He reached out for her and she caught his hand in hers and kissed it.

"Eyes only. We will start with one sense at a time, our eyes."

His jaw snapped shut with the effort, but he complied and draped his arm casually over his hip.

Katherine took a full inventory of his front. His chest, which she'd only managed to glimpse at the gym, was toned and muscled. His clothing hid the underlying bulk well. She had no doubt he could pick her up with one arm, that he could do anything he wanted to her.

Little trickles of excitement dripped down her thighs.

She'd already taken the full measure of his face, but she explored his eyes again. He was looking at her stomach, maybe her thighs, maybe the triangle of hair between her legs. He stopped himself just as he almost touched her breast.

"No touching, right," he said. "They are just the perfect size." He made a cupping shape out of his palm. "Not too big, not too little."

"Just right?" she asked, suppressing a giggle.

"More than just right. Perfection."

His stomach was flat. Ripped. That's what he was. Finely ripped in every sense of the word.

She had thought his cock was fully erect when he stood naked before her, but she had been wrong about that. He grew steadily as she studied him. As they studied each other. He was almost as thick as her wrist, and the tip reached to his belly-button.

She swallowed hard, her jaw aching in antic-ipation.

She wanted to reach out and run her finger along the thick ridge facing her, to bend over him and wrap her lips around his tip and taste him for the first time. She breathed out steadily to keep herself from acting on impulse and continued her inventory of his body.

His legs were all masculine, tightly muscled and hairy.

That sensation that had overtaken her in the bar the first night was there again, but different, a deeper kind of knowing. Rather than the fuzzy dream-like inducing state of the other night, everything was in sharp focus. Every sensory detail was heightened. Every inch of her felt alive and energized.

"Turn over so I can look at your back."

She did as he told, fresh waves of excitement taking hold. Being told what to do was a nice change of pace. She stretched out so he could see every inch of her.

She breathed in deeply, quelling a sudden nervousness. After several minutes, he shifted on the bed.

"Your turn."

He turned away from her, giving her a complete view of his backside. He was tan all over. His buttocks were as deeply tanned as the rest of him. Naked sunbather then.

A small indentation above the cleft of his ass begged to be explored, kissed. She would tend to it at some point. Dead center along his spine, a faint white line stood in stark relief to the tanned skin.

It was old. Really, really old, but still noticeable. She reached out and ran her finger along the scar, forgetting about her own no touching rule. His shoulders clenched and goose bumps burst out all over his flesh.

"I broke my back when I was eight."

She shifted to her knees and gently pushed him onto his stomach. Straddling him across his thighs, she kissed the small of his back. Then, she ran her tongue along the scar all the way up to his neck. She moved upward so that she was now straddling him across his firm ass. Her mound pressing against the cleft.

He raised himself on his arms and twisted so he could see her. "I take it the just looking stage has passed?"

She worked her hands along his shoulders, down the broad delicious back.

"I want to touch every part of you."

"You're excited," he said. "You're dripping against my ass."

"Your cock is making a permanent impression in the mattress."

His laugh buzzed through her. She ran her hands up and down his spine, feeling him, touching him, memorizing the tiny little bumps.

Suddenly, she was on her back. He had flipped her onto her back without any effort at all and with a speed that left her breathless.

He pushed her legs open and knelt between them. He ran his hands up her legs from her knees to her pussy, his thumbs pulling at her outer folds to expose her completely to him. A sudden vulnerability rippled through her.

He paused and caught her eye. "Fingers okay?"

"Fingers are fine."

He licked his lips. "Mouth and tongue?"

"God yes. Please."

He moved forward and hovered over her in a push-up. Kissed her lips. "Can I kiss you after I eat you out?"

"Thanks for asking. Yes."

He rolled his eyes upward. "Good lord, you are amazing." He lowered himself onto her for a second so she could feel his cock against her belly.

He proceeded to kiss and lick her from her neck all the way down until his head was between her legs. He spread her wide open again, the cool air hitting her wet clit.

He nibbled at her inner thigh, licked her labia, teasing her without ever going straight for her throbbing button. He slid two fingers into her, slowly moved them in and curling them up against her g-spot. Finally, finally, he circled her clit with his tongue. He sucked it into his mouth, flicking it in rhythm with his fingers that tapped inside her. He fucked her with his fingers, as his tongue worked magic.

"Perfection, right there," she said, catching her breath as he continued his onslaught.

He didn't let up at all. If anything, his tongue became more persistent, working to ensure she would come any moment. Her hips twitched upward in counterpoint to his staccato thrusts against her clit.

Just as she was about to come. He stopped. He pressed the flat of his tongue against her, quelling her throbbing immediately and withdrawing his fingers.

Her eyes flew open and she rose up on her elbows. "What the? Why did you stop?"

"I'm not ready for you to come."

"I can come multiple times."

"Me too," he said grinning up at her. His chin was shiny with her juices.

She flopped back against the pillows. He moved upward to hover over her in standard missionary position. His cock hung down, fully engorged and beautiful, tapping against her pussy. So close, and yet...*Could she do it? Could she take him all? Katherine Agatha Joan O'Malley do NOT THINK of his dick inside you again.*

She palmed his balls and pressed her forearm against the length of his cock. She slid her palm along the underside of his smooth, velvety skin, wrapping her fingers around him. She stroked him, capturing his pre-cum with her thumb and using it as lube.

"Let me give you head," she said, licking her lips.

He flipped onto his back and she climbed onto him, her wet pussy over his face, sixty-nine style.

He pushed two fingers into her, finger-fucking her again while she ran her tongue along his cock from stomach to tip. There was no way she could take him all in with her mouth. She slid her hand up and down around the base of his cock while circling the tip with her tongue around the tip of his cock. She engulfed as much of him as she could to give him an experience he'd never forget. She worked her head up and down with gusto, her only goal was to get him to come. She dropped all thoughts of her own pleasure, focusing solely on making him explode.

She could tell he was holding back, so she started to hum. She could feel the vibration from her throat through her hand. He took in a deep breath and relaxed, his hips began to move in rhythm with her head. His hands dropped to his side as he let go. His whole body tensed, and his back arched as he shot his hot load into her mouth. She licked at him until he stopped bucking underneath her.

He pulled her onto his face, and she let him guide her to straddle his face. It was one of her favorite positions, but one that freaked a lot of men out. Gerard seemed to be particularly good at finding her sweet spot. She made sure he had access to air as she ground her pussy into his face. His hands spread her ass cheeks wide as he lapped at her hungrily.

As she was about to come, he stopped all motion.

"Not again," she groaned, trying to find purchase against his mouth. "Please, keep going."

But he wouldn't let her. He was strong enough to easily lift her off and away from him, placing her on her back again. He turned onto his side and pulled at her nipples. "Not yet."

Her whole body pulsed with need. She had nearly come twice now, and both times he'd stopped, holding her back had left her wanting it even more.

She met his eyes. They twinkled with amusement. She hit him playfully on the shoulder. "You're doing this on purpose. You want me to beg for it, don't you?"

He pulled her nipple upwards and let go. The pinching release was exhilarating. He went back and forth, pinching, releasing, pinching, releasing. The tingling sensation between her nipple and her clit intensified with each pinch and release.

Her hips pushed upward with an intense desire. An overwhelming desire for him to fill her overcame her, a desire she'd never felt with a man in bed before. She was terrified and excited at the same time.

She wanted him *inside* her.

Needed him inside her.

She *had* to have his cock inside her.

"Oh. My. God. Gerard. I want you to fuck me."

He continued his nipple play, pinching and releasing. The pain and release felt exquisite, as if she were riding on the edge of a glassy wave.

"You want me to fuck you?"

"Yes, please."

He pinched her and released, then he stopped. "Let me get this straight. You want me to put my cock inside your pussy and fuck you."

She didn't want him to stop touching her, she needed release, but was willing to wait if it meant she could have more. She raised herself up on her elbows, her nipples red from the attention, her chest heaving. "Gerard. I've never asked anyone to do this before."

"Your rules were pretty clear...no fucking."

"It's okay. I want to feel you inside me. Just...go slow. Please, Gerard...Fuck me. Please." She lifted her hips, hungrily seeking pressure of any kind.

He pinched her nipples one last time and raised himself over her in missionary position.

He teased her, pressing the head of his cock against her clit then touched the opening of her dripping pussy. She arched her hips toward him, eager to take him in one inch at a time. He pulled away just as she thought he would enter her.

"Nope. Your rules. Not going to break them no matter how much you beg me."

He pressed his shaft against her clit and gently thrust against the folds of her vagina.

His cock against her like this was delicious, it was almost like having him inside her, wasn't it? She wanted him inside her, but she wouldn't beg him again. She was so close to coming, anyway. He slid his cock along her clit from tip to base, covering himself in her slick juices. He ground into her, completely on the outside, finding her sweet spot over, and over, and over.

The sensation threw her over the edge, and she screamed his name when he finally let her come.

atherine slept through the night in Gerard's arms. It felt natural, like the place she was supposed to be. She woke up early and didn't have the heart to wake him, he looked so peaceful sleeping like that. She found a piece of paper and wrote him a note telling him she had a running date and would see him later.

Her mom was still asleep when she got in, but appeared at the front door before Katherine could sneak back out in her running gear.

"I didn't want to wake you." She leaned over to tie her shoe-laces so her mom couldn't see her face.

"You didn't come home last night. I'm surprised. You were practically falling apart the other night about this man kissing some girl in the gym, and then, all of a sudden, you're spending the night with someone. Is this the same man?"

"I should have let you know I wasn't going to be home. I hope I didn't worry you." She pushed her way past her mom. "I'll be back in an hour."

Her mom grabbed her by the arm. "Katherine, you are thirty years old. I don't have a problem with you having sex. I just would have appreciated a text letting me know your plans."

Katherine briefly met her eyes. There was no judgment there. Just Mom being Mom.

She wanted to ask her mom and get her opinion about Gerard, but she couldn't talk to her mom about sex or relationships. Not after what she'd learned about her dad and certainly not after the night she'd had. But, why was she still here? She'd rarely stayed more than a couple of days before. What if this break was something more permanent?

"When are you going home?" she blurted out.

Her mother's lips twisted together as if she were holding something in. She straightened her shoulders and shook her head. "I don't know, Katherine. I am sorry to be such an inconvenience to you. I will stay out of your way best I can."

Katherine watched her in silence as she disappeared into the guest room.

Katherine started off her jog feeling bad about trying to get rid of her mom. She pounded the pavement, oblivious to the rest of the world around her.

She slowed to a jog as she hit the river trail. The Cherry blossoms had burst open into cheerful pink dots brightening the landscape. She stopped underneath a particularly glorious branch and ran her finger along a row of the delicate petals and breathed in the heady scent. They were the smell of pure, unadulterated spring. She almost didn't even notice when Kenny joined her at their usual meeting place.

"Whoa, girl, you are in another world. What's going on?"

Katherine wasn't sure how to explain things to him. Kenny had never fully understood her steadfast refusal to go all the way with the men she dated. But, then again, he couldn't get pregnant.

"Gerard."

"You must be happy it's not Jerry. I was going to text you, but I had to see your face when you said it."

"Haha. Funny. The guy you never gave me the background check on."

"I was gonna get back to you on that. I had a little emergency of the kind that pays so well, so I got interrupted. What I do know is that he was a child prodigy. Early graduate. Stellar performance in school. All pretty boring stuff. I can keep digging if you want."

"No need. I know who he is. And, my office did a thorough background check on him already."

"Well, was I off base?"

Katherine laughed. "I actually haven't read it all either. I saw his picture and closed the file because I recognized him as my guy from New York."

"So, what's the problem, sweetie?"

"I spent the night with Gerard."

Kenny turned towards her so fast, she almost tripped over him. "Oh. MY. GOD. Did you? You did the deed, didn't you? You finally did it!" Kenny was giddy with excitement. He actually jump-skipped a few steps while pumping his fist in the air.

"Calm down. And no. We didn't. Not exactly."

"Seriously? What do you mean not exactly?"

"I wanted to. Kenny, that's what's freaking me out. I have never, ever, wanted to do it like this."

"You have some of the stupidest rules I have ever heard of."

"They're not stupid. They've kept me from getting pregnant. And I've never gotten any STDs either."

Kenny held up a hand. "Fine. Fine. But what happened? I can tell by looking at you that you're upset."

"I begged him to fuck me, Kenny. I begged him to do it. And he refused."

Kenny stopped abruptly. It was like his feet couldn't work when his mind was working on something so incomprehensible.

She slowed and jogged back to him.

He stared at her, his jaw practically on his chest. "Let me get this straight. You actually begged a man to actually fuck you as in actually put his cock inside you? And he actually said 'no.'?"

"I almost came twice Kenny, he held me off. I swear to God, it was so hot. All I could think about was him inside me, filling me up."

"And he didn't fuck you?" Kenny's jaw hung open.

"He told me he was following my rules, and he refused to break them in the heat of the moment."

"What happened?"

"I had him on his stomach and was massaging his back. Then, he just flipped over, and moved me like I didn't weigh anything. He was on top of me. and we were just all over the place. I was giving him head, and something inside me just came alive. A desire to feel him inside me, to take all of him in."

"He didn't just jump on you as soon as you asked him to...?" Kenny made a crude gesture with his fingers.

She back-slapped him weakly. "Don't be such a

dork. And, no. That's the thing. He totally could have. He was doing this thing where he was teasing me-- pulling and pinching my nipples."

Kenny fanned himself. "Go on."

"Seriously? I'm not telling you this to get you off."

"Fine. Fine." He adjusted his posture to show some respect. "So, he was teasing your nipples....and then?"

"He just played with me until I was..." she felt heat in her cheeks. "I begged him to do it. And then he wouldn't. He made me come without actually fucking me."

"And you're upset because he *didn't* fuck you?"

Katherine closed her eyes. "Yeah...maybe...."

Kenny crossed his arms. "Let me get this straight. You tell a guy you have strict rules. You try to break those rules and the guy says nope. Then, he proceeds to do whatever until you are screaming in ecstasy. I'm not seeing a problem here."

"I thought he actually didn't want to fuck me," Katherine said weakly.

"Of, for fuck's sake, Katherine. You know he totally wanted to. Being mad at someone for following your rules is stupid. He was just protecting himself and maybe honoring you. Did you think of that?"

"I feel like an idiot. There I was, telling him I never have sex with anyone. And then, an hour later I am totally begging him to do it to me."

"Yeah. Well, you were taken off guard. So... Did he get off at all?"

"Of course he did." Katherine's jaw still hurt. She rubbed it without thinking. "Three times."

Kenny moaned in appreciation. "Oh hell. Kat, how big is he?"

Katherine started running again. "Huge, Kenny. Huge. You'd be gaga over him." She held up her hands indicating a general size that may have been a little bit of an exaggeration.

He groaned and picked up the pace. "You are so cruel." He stuck his hands down his shorts and adjusted things. "You know how hard it is to run with a hard-on? But, ohh I like him already. You set rules, and he followed them. All you have to do is talk to the man, when you are stone-cold sober--or before you get all naked-- and I bet he's inside you fast as shit."

She bit her lower lip and breathed in fast.

Kenny examined her, grabbing her by the shoulders and turning her face to the light. He let out a long slow whistle. "Holy shit. He's the one, isn't he?"

Katherine's heart hammered in her chest even though they were standing still. "I've never...wanted to do it like that before."

"I know, sweetie, I know." Kenny put a comforting hand on her shoulder.

They started running again, and Katherine

couldn't help but wonder. When would they talk? What would she say? Was she willing to give up her strict rules and let him fuck her properly? So many rules she'd set up for herself that she was suddenly willing to break. She was pretty sure he hadn't had a vasectomy. Did she trust him enough to do it?

Chapter 22

Kenny was right. There wasn't anything preventing her from talking to Gerard about changing her rules now that she knew she wanted more from him. Part of a good relationship is being able to talk about things.

Her body buzzed with the thought of Gerard's body poised over hers. The way he had withheld himself to follow her rules was intoxicating. And infuriating. Any other man would have plunged on in. His denial of her had set her on fire. Made her even hungrier for him.

G: I don't like waking up alone.

K: I think we need to talk about those rules of mine before we see each other again.

G: The part where you tell me I am forbidden to do certain things and then you drive me insane by begging me to do the exact things you told me I couldn't do?

K: :(Yeah. Sorry about that. I've never wanted to before.

G: You've never begged anyone to fuck you before?

K: Never really wanted it like that.

G: I thought you were playing a game.

Katherine paused and thought about that. It could certainly have come across as a mind game. "Don't do that, whatever I say...oops...never mind! Please do."

K: I swear, no games. I have never broken my own rules.

G: You really want to?

K: Still do, yes.

G: You know what I would do to you if we were in the same room right now?

K: No, what?

G: I'd spank you.

Katherine re-read his text three times. Solidly confused and newly excited.

K: Spank me? Srsly? Why?

G: Because you were very naughty for trying to get me to break your rules.

K: I wasn't trying to get you to break them.

G: Sure you were. You deserve a solid spanking.

K: No one has ever spanked me before.

G: Right.

K: Seriously. I really meant the no intercourse thing.

G: Hard to believe. You're awfully competent in bed.

K: We both had fun, right?

G: Some of the hottest sex I've never had.

K: Me too. I've never had so many orgasms.

G: I love the way you practically bend in half when you come.

K: So, if you were here right now, what would you do to me?

G: I'd spank you.

K: Not that again.

G: I'd spank you harder for questioning me.

Oddly enough, this little threat of his was turning her on.

She'd had a few guys ask to be spanked, but she'd never been into that end of it. The thought of Gerard spanking her, on the other hand was...sending warm tingles through her body. Of course, the thought of Gerard doing anything to her would probably do that.

Warmth flooded her sex in a way it shouldn't half an hour before the second day of hearings in front of some of the most esteemed members of Congress.

She fanned herself.

K: And what, exactly, do you think spanking me will accomplish?

G: A reminder that you're not in charge.

K: And what would you do after you spank me?

G: Kat, I want to fuck you like there's no tomorrow.

K: So you'll spank me and plunge that giant cock of yours into me?

G: Of course not. I'll warm you up first. We'll go slow. I've scared women off.

K: I can see why. I'm not scared.

G: We can go slow. Wait as long as you like.

K: I want you to fuck me right this minute.

G: I do to. Might be kinda awkward given I'm in the security line to get into your building.

K: LOL. Later. Tonight?

G: Are you sure?

K: Absolutely.

G: Spank and fuck. Tonight.

KATHERINE GOT INTO HER OFFICE, and Cheyenne was already waiting for her, plate of something sweet in her hand. "This is rhubarb coffee cake. "

Katherine shoved her phone into her pocket, she turned red just thinking about all the naughty conversation they were having, before she'd even had her first cup of coffee. "Oh, man. That looks delicious."

"I saw you have four BINGO spots. Are you going

to win it by going out with that CIA guy tonight?" Cheyenne asked.

Katherine had almost forgotten about the damned BINGO game and her date. She was so concerned about what was going on with Gerard, she couldn't even think of going out with another guy. Couldn't think about it and didn't want to kiss anyone else. Ever again.

How quickly things could change. Twenty-four hours before, she was ready to sneak out for a kiss to win. But Gerard changed that all last night by making her stick to her own rules. She couldn't quite wrap her head around all of it.

She felt a pang of guilt. There was no way she could go out with Ryan. Not when she had a date with Gerard. A date that would change everything for her. She wanted to explore a relationship with him, even more so than winning the trip. She put down the pile of papers she'd been gathering in her arms.

"Cheyenne," she said, "I'm going to give you my date with Ryan from the CIA tonight. I'm supposed to text him where to meet. But, I am not going to go."

Cheyenne gaped at her. "Seriously? You're just giving me your CIA guy?"

"Yeah. I'm just giving you my CIA guy."

"But you would have won."

"Won what?" Carleen asked.

They'd been so intent on their conversation that neither had seen her standing in the doorway.

"We're trying to figure out who is going to win that trip with Congressman Pierce," Katherine said slowly. "It's just a little game we're playing, and I'm almost there. I just...don't feel like playing any more. It's taking too much of my spare time."

She hoped that would deflect Carleen from asking any further questions.

Cheyenne busied herself with piling a couple of binders in her arms.

"I hope this game you are playing is not something that will embarrass Lincoln?"

Katherine dropped a binder and bent to pick it up. She could not look into Carleen's eyes and lie. It couldn't be done. She had an amazing ability to see through any subterfuge.

"Of course not," Katherine said, head still down. "We'd never do anything that would reflect poorly on the congressman."

Katherine took her time picking up the binder. When she straightened back up, Carleen stood in the doorway, blocking both her and Cheyenne from escape. She crossed her arms over her chest and examined them closely over the top rims of her glasses. A cold chill wormed its way down Kat's spine.

THE HEARINGS SLOWED DOWN to a crawl. She went back and forth between wanting to cancel with Gerard and wanting to jump all in. She'd spent so much time saying no, holding to her line, that this new desire for him scared her. It had happened so fast. But she wanted him in a way she had never wanted anyone else. A deep bond between them had taken root on Friday night. Everything about him told her she could trust him. Her whole body was electrified with anticipation.

She kept slipping back into a lulling daydream about Gerard and his naked body draped across the bed. His hands all over her body. His mouth everywhere. This was all more intense, more real than anything she'd ever experienced before. Had she really been strong all these years, keeping men at bay, forcing her rules on them? Or had some deep inner part of her she still didn't understand just been waiting?

Her mom texted asking if she would be home for dinner. When she told her she wouldn't be, that she would be spending the night at Gerard's place and not to expect to see her until the following evening, her mom's terseness came through clear in her text response. "Fine." Even her mom's sulking couldn't dampen Katherine's mood.

Gerard sat in on the rest of the hearing even though he'd testified the day before. At lunch time, he grabbed her by the hand and led her down to the same abandoned hallway she'd taken him to the day before.

"I had to see you. Face-to-face, to make sure you're still wanting to go through with tonight."

Katherine held his face in her hands. His beautiful eyes were questioning. "I had no idea I would change my mind. There was no game playing."

He relaxed visibly. "Okay. I believe you. Come over whenever you're done. No sneaking out on me this time."

"I left a note." There was no way she was going to sneak out in the middle of the night after making love for the first time in...well...really making love ever. Was that what this was? This giddy lightness? This strange hopeful excitement?

He slid his hands down her back to her ass, giving it a good squeeze and a playful pat. "I can't wait to punish you for being such a tease."

She weakened at the knees and collapsed into him from the unexpected jolt of need that coursed through her. "If I didn't have to go back into that hearing, I'd beg you to fuck me right here, right now."

He slid a hand up her skirt, his fingers probing into her wet slit. He slowly withdrew his fingers along her clit and pressed them back into her again. "You're ready for tonight, aren't you baby?"

She groaned into his mouth as he kissed her. She fell back against the wall for support as he toyed with her.

"Maybe we should do it right here. Maybe I should pull my cock out and fuck you while we're both fully dressed, a quickie against the wall."

She clenched around his hand as he increased speed and pressure. She could feel her body getting ready to release, and just as she was about to come, he stopped and pressed the flat of his palm against her throbbing clit.

He pulled his hand away and licked his fingers slowly. He slid the cardkey to his room into her bra. "I don't want you coming again until my cock is buried deep inside you..."

Chapter 23

The afternoon crept by. Every single second felt like an eternity as her clit throbbed, aching for release. She could have sworn the clock behind the hearing panel moved backward in the late afternoon. It wasn't until six-thirty that she managed to escape work. She couldn't help but smile the whole way to Gerard's hotel. Traffic was shitty, shittier than normal, and all she had was smiles. She pinched herself to make sure she was really awake. She still felt that painful wanting she'd first experienced with Gerard—the need to take him inside her. The craving was so strong it scared her.

She opened the door to wondrous smells emanating from the small kitchen. The day before, it had been the pristine, rarely used kitchen of a hotel used by people who reheat their leftovers in the microwave. Now, every heater thingy on the stove had a pot on it, and steam escaped around the edges.

It was obviously complicated and exotic, and certainly not something her mother would cook. In spite of the obvious flurry of cooking taking place, Gerard was nowhere to be seen.

"Gerard?" she called. When she used the French pronunciation of Gerard, it was sexy.

She stopped in the middle of the room and heard the shower running. She considered joining him, but decided against it. Shower sex always looked more fun than it was. Well, she'd have sex with Gerard anywhere, but for her first time, she wanted to luxuriate in his bed.

She wandered over to the stove and lifted one of the lids. Inside was some dark red delicious smelling chili or something—no, not chili. It smelled unlike anything she'd ever had before. She found a spoon and tasted it. Her eyes watered. It was spicier than she'd expected. Unusual flavors burst in her mouth. She tried to suss them out, but wasn't quite sure what they were.

She lifted another lid. Cardamom and garlic wafted out from what appeared to be cabbage, potatoes, and carrots in a rich buttery sauce. She found a spoon and gave the pot a good stir.

The third pot contained some kind of greens pungent with garlic and ginger.

The last burner--burner that's what those are called-- of the stove had a steamer basket. Thick pancakes were neatly rolled up side by side. Their sour smell was rich and heady.

"Ever have Ethiopian food before?"

Katherine jumped. "Uhm...no? Don't think so."

She turned around to find Gerard standing behind her in a bathrobe. "Dinner first. You'll need your strength."

"Will I now?" she smiled, slightly disappointed he wasn't ripping off his robe and carrying her into the bedroom right that second. He seemed to have an agenda planned. She'd just go with it.

"I didn't make it too spicy. But, I'm betting you can take the heat," Gerard said as he ladled small portions of everything onto two plates.

"You know, I don't cook at all," Kat said.

"Good thing I am a master at it."

"Uhm...Gerard, I don't see any forks." She felt around her plate in case it was under the rim.

"You use your hands. The pancake is actually injera—the national bread. You pick up the stew—it's called sik sik wat--with the injera, like this." He ripped off a piece of the bread and wrapped it around a piece of something dark red on his plate. "Open."

The command sent a shiver of anticipation through her. Open...Oh, how she wanted to open everything to him. To expose herself fully to this amazing man.

She opened her mouth, and he fed her the bite. New flavors burst across her palette. It was unlike anything she'd ever had. Spicy, intense, and robust. She'd never eaten Ethiopian cuisine before, but if Gerard's cooking was any indication she knew she would be searching out the local restaurants soon.

"How do you know so much about all this?" she asked waiving her hands over the plates.

"My best friend growing up was Ethiopian. His mom was a fantastic cook, and she taught me everything. Even how to make Injera...But that takes a few days. I bought this at a market."

Katherine felt her heart swell. She'd never had a man cook for her like this before.

She got the hang of eating the food without covering her fingers in the sauces pretty quickly. It was tempting to eat every bite on her plate, it was that good.

When they were done with dinner, Gerard held out his hands to her. "Let's take a bath."

The water she'd heard earlier was actually the bathtub. He'd started it before she got there because it was big enough for the two of them and some friends. Gerard poured a bottle of something foamy and lavender scented into the bath as it finished filling.

He kissed her on the neck and slowly undressed her, batting her hands away any time she tried to help. He took his time, caressing her neck with his lips. Nibbling at her earlobes. Running his fingers along her naked spine. Once she was completely naked, he stood back and looked at her.

"Turn around for me."

She did as she was told, her body aching for his touches.

"Beautiful."

He slipped his robe off and helped her into the tub.

Kat breathed in the lavender as she sunk into the depths of the tub, her whole body relaxing into Gerard as he settled in behind her.

He wrapped his arms around her and she laid back to rest against him. He cradled her body with his as he washed her hair. His fingers were gentle yet firm as he ran them through her scalp. Every touch made her body burn with hunger for more.

All tension left her body as he tended to her. He worked all the kinks out of her shoulders, her back, her neck. As his hands did their magic, she could feel his erection growing against her back, reminding her of what was to come. Soon, she hoped.

Everything shifted as her entire body became relaxed and receptive to his touches. He lifted her out of the tub and dried her off. He carried her to the bed all wrapped in huge fuzzy towels. She rolled onto her side and watched as he finished drying himself off.

"Are you ready, my love?" he asked.

<hr>

"AS READY AS I'll ever be."

He leaned over her, kissing her on the lips.

"Spread your legs," he ordered.

She did as she was told. He knelt on the bed, strad-dling one of her legs and slicked a finger with her juices. He teased her with it, sliding it slowly inside her pussy and dragging it along her clit like he had during lunch.

She closed her eyes and pushed her hips up toward the contact.

The palm of his hand caught at her mound and pushed her against the bed. "Open your eyes and look at me."

She was almost overcome by a strange near-hypnotic state as their eyes locked.

"Two now," he said.

She felt a little more pressure as he finger-fucked her with two fingers.

"Three."

She groaned as he continued to press inside her, to prepare her for him.

"You're so wet. You want me, don't you?"

She moaned in agreement. Words were suddenly beyond her. She had given up any and all agendas of her own and was letting him do whatever he wanted. She trusted him, and she wanted him. Needed him. Her entire body pulsed with her need.

He stroked her slowly, twisting his hand around with each motion.

"So, Katherine, tell me. What do you want right now?"

She wasn't sure she could talk, she moaned something incoherent.

"You have to say it."

She thought she said, "are you kidding me" but it came out a completely garbled mess.

He laughed, his thumb tweaking her clit as his fingers continued their twisting inside her. "Seriously. You can manage, *Please, Gerard, fuck me now.*"

His commanding voice buzzed through her body. "I'm about to come," she gasped.

He stopped all motion, leaving his fingers inside

her. "So, you can speak. And, no. You won't. Not until I tell you you can."

She breathed in deeply. "Please, let me come," she begged.

"No, Katherine. I told you, you won't come until I am inside you. So, be specific. What do you want?"

She sucked in a deep breath and met his eyes. They drilled into her, gave her the support she needed to say it aloud. "Please. Gerard. Please. Fuck. Me. Fuck. Me. Fuckmefuckmefuckmefuckme." The words became a mantra.

"Why didn't you ask before?" His smile was bright and wide, teasing, and she wanted to slap him and kiss him all at the same time.

He leaned over and rummaged in the drawer before flopping onto his back. "We should start with you on top. So you're in control."

He lifted her over him until she knelt, straddling him and handed her the condom. She ripped it open and rolled it down his cock, cupping his balls gently in her hand. She stroked him a few times before taking him by the base and guiding the tip of his cock into her.

His fingers had done a little to warm her up, but his cock was thicker. Thicker than any toy she owned. She lowered herself gradually onto him, feeling the widest part press at her all around, spreading her little by little, her pussy adjusting to his girth an inch at a time.

He sucked in his lower lip as she took her time. He didn't move, but let her adjust to him at her pace. He was obviously holding back his own need for release. She marveled that his cock could even fit inside her. The mirror behind the headboard gave her an excellent view of his rock hard dick moving into her as she continued her descent in agonizingly slow motion.

She savored her progress down his shaft with a reverent awe until she'd engulfed him completely. She settled onto him, concentrating on the sensation of having Gerard inside her at last. She tilted her head back and let out a long, slow, satisfied moan. He was inside her. All of him. She squeezed against him, trying to make contact with every part of him she could.

"You feel amazing," she said.

"So do you." He reached up and caressed her neck, tracing a line down across her breast and stomach to the point where their flesh became one. "You fit perfectly."

She clenched around him, reveling in the moment. She'd waited so long, not even realizing she wanted it, not understanding that being with the right person would make the difference. What she had needed was him. She felt whole. Complete.

"Okay," she said at last. "Let's get moving."

Slowly, she rocked back and forth against him, feeling the entire length of him inside her. Every movement was exquisite. But now, she wanted all of him, and she was ready. She lifted up, but not completely off, stopping just at the very tip of his cock before dropping down full hilt. She found the motion, the exact tilt of her hip that set her clit on fire. She rode him, taking what she needed from him, one stroke, one movement at a time. Each small thrust added to the last. She came, squeezing hard around him, and collapsed onto his chest with him still inside her fully erect.

He wrapped his arms around her pulling him close, demanding nothing.

He had been holding back, watching her enjoy him and taking nothing from her. She shifted as a second wave of her orgasm trilled through her.

"I think I'm in love," she whispered.

"I've been in love with you since the moment I saw you."

Do you believe in love at first sight?

She gave herself a minute to recover. It had been everything she'd imagined but better. The heat of his warm flesh inside her was the perfect and ultimate physical connection.

"You haven't come, have you?"

"I will. I wanted to watch you first. Are you ready, Kat?"

He flipped her onto her back into missionary and took his sweet time, pulling his cock out all the way and rubbing it along her clit before sliding it back inside. He teased her like this, the slow movement along her clit, and delving all the way in over and over until she was on the edge of another orgasm. She grabbed at his shoulders, wanting more from him.

"I'm close to coming again," she said. "Now, Gerard. Please, take me now. Don't hold anything back."

He plunged into her as she came. She could feel a release coming, like nothing she had ever experienced. Her pussy clenched around him. He thrust in and out as she continued to orgasm around him. It was his turn to take his fill of her. He gave way to the carnal needs of his body and fucked her hard. Fast.

She rode wave after wave of an orgasm that seemed to have no end. Or maybe it was ten different orgasms or fifty. She had no way of accounting for the way her body was reacting to him.

He groaned loudly, his cock buried deep, and held himself against her as he exploded inside her. "Katherine, Oh...God, Katherine..."

She clutched her legs around his back holding his

whole body close, keeping him there for as long as possible, squeezing herself around him.

He waited, letting her come down from her orgasm with him inside her, their eyes dancing together.

He pulled out and collapsed next to her, bringing her in close into his side.

She snuggled into him. He cradled her against him. "I've never experienced anything quite like that before," he said. He kissed the top of her head. "It just felt right. Like when we were dancing and seemed to understand every move of my hands and hips. Your body and mine were made for each other."

With her head against his chest, she could hear the steady rhythm of his heart beating. It couldn't have been more perfect.

▭

AFTER A WHILE, she stretched luxuriously, fully content and a little sleepy. Gerard nuzzled her neck and ears. He teased her nipple by pulling it up and away and letting it pop back into place. He climbed out of bed. She was ready for another round, and it looked like he was, too.

"I'm thirsty. Is there anything to drink?"

"Not just yet, sweetheart. There's a small matter we have to take care of first."

He lifted her out of bed. She wasn't sure what he was up to, but being in his arms like this was about the sexiest thing ever. She linked her arms around his neck and he kissed her on the lips. A hard, fast smack. Perfunctory.

She had completely forgotten about his promise to spank her. Had he really meant it?

He carried her to the end of the bed and dropped down onto the long ottoman.

Suddenly, she was face-down across his lap. He had maneuvered her body like she was a rag-doll.

"Gerard? What?"

"I owe you a spanking."

"Oh, you were kidding, right?"

"I was dead serious. I am going to spank you."

She laughed. "Are you serious? You are not going to spank me." She was suddenly awake, the post-sex languor swept away completely.

He ran his hand over her naked ass, smoothing over her buttocks, spreading her ass-cheeks wide. She instinctively clenched together, suddenly worried he was going somewhere they'd not talked about. But then he patted her bottom. Gently at first. A little pat here. Then there. Warming up her ass all around with light slaps.

A little "oh" escaped her lips as her bottom flared to

life and sent her pussy signals she had no problem understanding.

"Remind me. Why are you spanking me?"

"Because you are a tease. You told me no fucking and then begged me to fuck you."

Her head was spinning with desire. "Oh, but you could have."

"And give you what you wanted?"

He slapped her bottom harder and began to work in a two-handed rhythm, waking every inch of her body through the gentle drumming of his hands. He was a musician waking whole melodies in her body she had studiously ignored for ten years.

"It seems like you've done this before," she said. "You know what you're doing."

"Google, my sweet. There are tutorials for every-thing out there."

She wiggled her bottom under his hands. She had no idea spanking could be such a turn-on. She might not have thought of it on her own, but it made her pussy slick with excitement. With every touch, Gerard made her want him all the more.

She sucked in her breath as he ramped up the spanking. She felt his erection grow against her belly and moaned in desire. He slowed down the pace and stopped, a hand on both cheeks quelling the stinging and sending heat through her body.

She twisted her upper body so she could look at him. His eyes were focused on her ass and he was breathing heavily. He met her eyes and slapped her bottom hard one more time.

"Ready for round two?"

Chapter 24

Katherine stretched awake. She watched Gerard sleep for a few minutes as the pink and purple dawn crept in through the window and made everything glow. His face had grown a stubble overnight. She gently kissed the scruffy jaw, the scrape of it against her lips sent new tingles through her, she didn't want to wake him this early. She rolled out of bed. Life continued post-sex and so did her job.

She'd brought an overnight bag with her so she wouldn't have to rush home. She texted Kenny that she wouldn't be running. Of all people, Kenny would totally understand her missing their training session. Besides, her bottom hurt from the spanking she'd received and she had no desire to be bouncing around.

She'd had sex. REAL sex as people kept telling her

.Even though she'd had sex a few times when she was younger, this was so much better in comparison. Being crazy in love with the person she was having sex with made a huge difference, and the fact that she was completely comfortable with Gerard probably didn't hurt.

Before she'd instituted her no penetration policy, that was basically all she'd ever experienced—unsatisfying and mostly embarrassing quickies. Her sexual repertoire had expanded exponentially after that. The combination of long foreplay and oral sex with actual, honest to God fucking was better than the sum of the parts. She'd experienced a profound connection with Gerard, and the most intense orgasms of her life. Certainly being as experienced as she was had been part of the perfection.

After their second round of post-spanking-mind-blowing sex, they'd climbed out of bed to watch the latest episode of *Scandal.* Gerard ordered up a dessert with some champagne, and spoon fed her one glorious bite at a time. They'd gone back to bed to practice positions straight out of the Kama Sutra. They'd cuddled in each other's arms talking about ephemera until the wee hours of the morning. She felt like she knew him better than any other person in the world—including her Tri-Delts, Kenny, or any of her siblings.

She couldn't imagine a better life than coming

home to Gerard, making love, having a home-cooked meal, making love again, and falling into dreamy sleep every night. She could easily get used to that scenario.

She was sore but not in pain. Happy sore. Better than working out sore.

The shower was one of those fancy contraptions with a rainfall overhead, jets on the side, and a handheld thing. Water came at her from every direction. As she lathered her hair into thick foam, she wondered if Gerard would be interested in moving in with her and stopped herself short. For her, last night had been transformative. She had no doubt about the love that had overtaken her.

In love with Gerard. In love with each other. She wanted to hop back into bed and stay there forever. Lust and love mingled together. That's the way it's supposed to be, isn't it?

He could see her as just an interesting conquest, playing her after learning about her no penetration rule. *No penetration, my ass. Nailed her!*

No. He had said it was love at first sight. He had said he'd been in love. Calling her *my love.* This was real for both of them.

Still. It was all happening *so* fast. Even though she believed she knew him, there was still so much they needed to learn about each other.

She needed to tell him why she didn't want children. Maybe he wanted dozens. There had to be a conversation about this before long. Before she was in so deep she'd never climb out. If it wasn't too late already.

Maybe if he was awake, she could talk to him when she was done getting ready for her day. She had promised to not leave him without saying goodbye. What a sucky morning conversation. *Good morning, sweetheart. The reason I didn't want to fuck you is I don't want your babies.* It sounded so heartless and... sad to her.

She shoved away the sudden image of a baby Gerard that came to mind. A cute, cuddly little guy with his dark green eyes. *None of that, now.*

She scrubbed at her body, trying hard to not let any post-coital regret ruin the elation she had been feeling. They'd used condoms with some spermicide, so it was very unlikely she would get pregnant. Plus, she had the IUD. Besides, she was pretty regular, and she wouldn't be ovulating for another week.

They would make it work. She'd go on the pill. He'd get snipped. Unless he had always dreamed of having children. He'd asked her *how* she had avoided penetration sex for ten years, not *why*. She ran her fingers through her hair again. They'd talk about all this soon.

She walked out of the bathroom completely coiffed and dressed, ready for her day.

Gerard lay on his back, unaware that she had come back into the room, one arm stretched over his head and the other holding his phone. "Yeah, buddy, I know, I know. I am totally bummed I'll miss your game on Saturday. I'm staying in D.C. over the weekend. I'll be there for the next game though. Promise."

Katherine slipped on her shoes, puzzled by the conversation. Was he talking to his brother Carl?

"That's right, kiddo. Hey, put on Mommy, will you?"

Mommy? There was no way he'd call his mother *Mommy*. He couldn't be talking to Carl.

Katherine became a statue. Gerard had no idea she was standing there listening to his conversation.

"Hey. Sorry. I know. I thought this would just be a few days, too. Work is keeping me here. I haven't even started looking for a place to live. I want to find something in a good school district for Jake."

Katherine worked frantically to piece the words together.

Kiddo.

Mommy.

Jake.

School.

Each word hit her in the chest--a knife twisting into her heart.

Was he telling a wife a load of crap just so he could stay in D.C. with her for the weekend?

What. The. Actual. Fuck?

Katherine scanned his hand again. No ring on his finger. No tell-tale signs there ever was a ring on his finger.

She wanted to throw up. She needed to get as far away from him as possible. She stuffed her clothing willy-knilly into her bag. There wasn't enough air in the room, she had to get out.

Gerard clutched the phone to his chest. "Katherine? Hey, are you leaving?"

Her throat was so tight she couldn't get a word out.

She pointed to the phone.

His brow knit together and he looked at the phone in confusion before speaking into it again. "Hey, I need to call you back. Yeah. Sure. This afternoon works."

He swiveled to get out of bed. Kat held her hand up to stop him.

"You have a kid? Are you married?" She backed away from him.

Gerard's mouth dropped open, and he looked at her like he'd never seen her before.

"Married? What?" He looked down at his phone and back up at her, eyes going wide and shaking his head. "Oh. Ohhhhh...no...no... Katherine, this isn't what it looks like."

"It never is." She ran for the door.

Chapter 25

Katherine wasn't about to go home to her mother, so she grabbed a taxi to work. She went straight through security and up to her office. It was early yet, and no one had started coffee. She went through the motions, not really even wanting coffee, but doing something normal had a calming effect on her.

She had known it was too good to be true. It had been too perfect. Too magical. Too wonderful. Damn. How could she not have known he was married with a kid. Or was it more than one? She hadn't asked either —when would they have talked about kids? She was so hot and bothered to jump into the sack with him, that she didn't even find out if he understood and accepted her requirements.

She powered her phone off to make it easier to

ignore him. He'd already sent five texts she refused to open. What could he say to her? She was obviously just a conquest to him.

She couldn't face him until she had managed to tame the feelings roiling around inside. How had she been so fucking stupid? She was usually good at ferreting out the bullshit most men used to hide their relationships, their wives.

She refused to be the other woman. She wasn't like her mom; she didn't want to be anything like her. Mom was still at her apartment. Shit. If she continued down that path, is that what her life would be like? Would she forever be running away from men to avoid talking to them?

It was hard to focus on work while riding the relationship rollercoaster at warp speed. Thank God the hearings were over. She could hide in her office all day. She shut her door and pulled the blind on the small window for privacy.

She scanned her email. After about ten minutes she realized she had absolutely no memory of what she'd just read. One of the briefs needed to be copied for Carleen. Instead of passing it on to Cheyenne, she stood at the copy machine. It was about the only thing she could manage. Something mindless. Mind-numbing.

As she got into the rhythm of stacking papers she

tried to piece together anything Gerard had said over the last two days that would have given her any clue he was married and had a kid. What had she missed?

The one thing in the world she did not want--the one thing she couldn't handle--a man with a kid. The man she was in love with had a child he hadn't told her about.

She leaned back against the counter and closed her eyes. Things had gotten totally messed up.

Carleen came in with a pile of folders and stopped short. "Katherine, what are you doing in here? It's awfully early, even for you."

Katherine glanced at the clock. It wasn't even seven yet. "I was nearby. I figured I might as well get to work early."

"Since you're here...I need to talk to you about this ridiculous Bingo game."

The words almost didn't register right away. Carleen raised her hand in front of Katherine's face and waved it back and forth. The strange trance-like desperation she'd been feeling ever since hearing Gerard talk to his wife and son shattered and was replaced with the sudden realization that Carleen knew about the game.

"Katherine, did you hear me? Hello?"

"Game?" she asked, hoping to buy a few seconds of time.

"So, it's true."

Kat never knew how Carleen got all her information, but it was useless to deny anything at this point. "Yes."

Carleen slapped the folders down on the counter. "What in the world do you think you're playing at? Whose fool idea was this, anyway?"

Katherine shrugged. Madeline was not a close friend, but there were some rules when it came to office politics. This was not a capital crime, and there was no way she was going to snitch on her co-workers for something that would blow over in a day or two anyway. "It was just something that came up at the bar last week."

"Last week...When you all took Chloe out?"

"Yeah. You were there." Katherine hesitated. "With that intern from Senator Hart's office."

Carleen raised an eyebrow.

Katherine held up her hands. "That wasn't a threat or anything. Just a comment. To help you remember when it was."

"But you're documenting everything on Instagram with check-ins? Putting a photo of yourself on social media and tagging the other women in the game? Linking you all to each other?"

"Yes. But the guys don't know they're part of the game. They're just...you know...there. We don't post their photos or anything like that."

"And the purpose of this game is to determine who goes with the Congressman to the meeting in Vegas?"

Katherine nodded.

"I see you've checked in at four places."

"It was just a fun way to decide who goes. There's no harm meant by it."

"You were told to decide who goes to this meeting. You could have rolled dice. Drawn straws. Put your names in a hat. Or decided who would go based on merit. No. Instead, you decide to draw men into a kissing game?" Carleen held her hands up on either side of her head, fingers spread wide and closed her eyes. She breathed in deeply and looked suddenly calmer when she opened her eyes again.

"You realize I am going on that trip?"

Katherine didn't see where this sudden change in tack was going. "Yeah?"

"So, I am going to need someone I can trust holding the fort down for me, here. That, my dear, is a much better career booster than being his aide at this meeting. Sure, being present at the meeting will be a little boost to someone, but you all have blown this way out of proportion by turning it into a competition like this."

Katherine wasn't sure she saw it that way.

"Think about it Katherine. If you are here taking over my job for that week, you will be forging the path for taking over my job permanently. I'm not going to be here forever. As a matter of fact, I don't want to be here when he starts his presidential election bid."

Katherine had imagined Lincoln running for office, but with Carleen at the helm of the machine getting him there. The office would be a completely different place without Carleen, and Kat wasn't quite sure she wanted to step into the other woman's shoes that directly.

"Stunts like this could get him and you laughed out of office."

"You're being overly-dramatic. People play stupid games all the time. This is Washington D.C."

"You will not let this continue. I'm counting on you to shut this thing down. I don't want Lincoln to find out about this, and I don't want anyone outside the office to either. God forbid the press gets hold of it."

"It looks like we're doing touristy stuff."

"Don't make me doubt the decision to have you as my replacement. If this gets out? You'll all be fired. And, I don't care if your dad is best friends with the congressman, your ass will be history. Do I make myself clear?"

"Crystal. I'll take care of it, Carleen."

"Make sure you do." Carleen stopped at the doorway, her eyes narrowing on Kat. "You don't seem too terribly upset about me finding out about this."

"I've got some other things on my mind." Katherine bit back tears and looked away. She didn't want her to think she was crying because of Carleen coming down hard on her for the game.

"Why in the world are you about to cry? I'm not that scary. Fess up."

Carleen knew her better than anyone else in the office did. Katherine had always had a hard time explaining her problems with kids, but Carleen knew her history. She'd understand.

"One of the guys I met over the weekend. He's married and has a kid, but I didn't know it. I spent the night with him last night, and he was talking to them on the phone when I came out of the bathroom."

Carleen tilted her head, eyes narrowing on Katherine. "Wait. You mean the guy from the hearing yesterday? Gerard? Gerard Porter?"

Carleen never forgot a name or a face. Just one of her many attributes Lincoln Pierce counted on. She followed him around at gatherings, whispering in his ear, reminding him of important names and events.

"That's him."

Carleen shook her head. "I handed you his background check before the hearing on Wednesday. Did you even look at it?"

Katherine couldn't picture anything other than his photo and his name. "No. Actually. I was so shocked to see him there, I didn't read the whole thing." Kenny's background check hadn't dredged up a child or wife.

"He's not married. Never has been. I don't know what he said that made you think that. He does have a kid...I think going into kindergarten next fall. But, he's not married. I think you should look at the file again."

"If he's not married, why would he have been saying the things he was saying?"

"Maybe you took it the wrong way? Think it through."

"But he has a kid. That's the real deal breaker for me."

"Why, Katherine? I know you've always said you don't want kids, but I thought it was because you hadn't found the guy to have them with."

"You know my family as well as anyone."

"I do. But you're so close to your brothers and sisters."

"All nine of them. They're like my own kids. I practically raised them."

Carleen's brow furrowed in consternation. "Maybe that's the problem. They aren't your kids. Besides, being a step-mom to a five-year-old is totally different, no one is expecting you to raise them."

"I don't know what it takes to get this through to people. I am not going to be anyone else's mother."

"Your obsession over this kid thing is neurotic. Maybe you should get some therapy."

Katherine looked away. Was she neurotic? She ended most of her dates with a simple, unproductive, kiss good-night. There had never been the heat, the zing, *that thing* she'd experienced with Gerard.

With Gerard, there had been an ineffable bond between them from the moment he'd placed a martini in front of her. The previous night had been more than she had dreamed and almost overwhelming in its sheer perfection.

Carleen patted her on the shoulder. "Kill the game. Remember you're just getting to know this guy. His kid isn't a big part of the picture just yet, and dumping him before you even meet his son is immature, and frankly, beneath you."

Chapter 26

Katherine managed to pull herself together with the morsel of knowledge that Gerard was not married. There was that at least. He had sent the first text shortly after she left him. Then another every hour. They were variants of wondering what was going on. What had he done? Was she okay? What was wrong? Could he come see her at her office?

He wasn't blowing her off, he was doing the opposite. She didn't know what to think.

Later in the day, Cheyenne cornered her in the bathroom to talk about Harrison to tell her what had happened at the Capitol Bar and Grill the night before. Gordy, the lobbyist from that shark firm Porter and Associates and Harrison almost got into a fight. Then, she whispered conspiratorially, Harrison left with Chloe. Cheyenne described the way they had looked at each other as they left the bar, she was pretty sure *that look* would lead to sex.

Katherine sighed heavily as she looked at herself in the mirror. There was a twinge of jealousy. She wished her romantic relationships could be a simple as Chloe's. She wished she didn't have to deal with this level of drama. And Harrison. She couldn't believe that he'd gone overboard with her suggestion to pretend to date.

She had assumed Harrison would play along with her suggestion they date as a cover. The last thing she had expected was for them to fall for each other. As they left the bathroom, and headed back to the office, Katherine noticed Madeline in the copy room.

She pulled Cheyenne into the room, and, to the surprised look of Madeline, shut the door.

Looking at Madeline, Katherine said, "Carleen found out about the game and is pissed. We need to shut it down."

"How'd she find out about it?"

"It doesn't matter. She overheard someone talking and started asking questions."

Cheyenne shook her head. "I am this close to winning. I just have one more to go."

"Drop the game."

Madeline crossed her arms. "You're so close with four kisses, just one more."

"I don't care. I'll stay here."

Madeline looked at her with suspicion. "Why would you drop out? I thought you wanted to keep Eleanor from going to this meeting."

"Things got complicated with Gerard. Winning this game means nothing to me anymore."

"Right. I believe that," Madeline said. She paused and looked at her with a fierceness that made Katherine take a step back. "Carleen is making too big of a deal out of a little game."

"Are you going to tell her that?" Katherine asked. "Seriously, you go tell Carleen she's blowing things out of proportion."

"I'm going to keep playing," Cheyenne said, interrupting them. "I have one more spot to get, so I'll win."

"Like hell," Madeline said. "You still have two to go."

Cheyenne frowned, counting up her dates on her fingers. "No. This is five."

"You took two guys to the same monument. One of them doesn't count."

Cheyenne dropped her head back. "Oh, man? I thought I had this."

Katherine held up her hands. "Look. If you want to keep playing, that's on you, but you can't do it with the check-ins. Make sure you do it privately. And, take me out of the game. Now. I am done. I will let the rest of the team know individually."

She opened the door and turned back to the other women. "I am totally serious. I am out. And I don't want to see or hear anything more about it."

She found Eleanor and Opal at their desks. Eleanor responded like Madeline and Cheyenne. She wasn't concerned about losing her job. It wasn't as though anyone was handing out state secrets on their dates.

Opal tilted her head to one side considering the situation. "Carleen's not going to fire anyone over this game. She just likes to make herself sound bigger than she is. She yields a lot of power with Lincoln, but he is reasonable and would probably see it as a waste of time more than anything."

Katherine wondered about Opal's actual mousiness. There was something more to this woman than she could define. Even after working with her for six years, she hardly knew her.

"It's during off hours," Katherine said.

"But not really. Don't you use your office contacts, information you only have because of the job you do, to get a date with Ryan?"

"How did you know about Ryan?" Katherine asked.

Opal shrugged. "I know everything that goes on

around here. Just because I am quiet doesn't mean I am not observant."

Katherine had a new respect for Opal. Katherine went back to her office only realizing Opal had never actually said anything about her involvement in the game.

She turned on her phone, bracing herself for incoming texts. Gerard had texted a total of twelve times since she'd turned off her phone, the last one just ten minutes before she turned on her phone. A creeping sense of embarrassment prevented her from responding to him. She'd made the assumption he was married and accused him of having an affair with her. The image of him standing next to the bed, naked and a "what the fuck" look on his face was seared into her memory.

She hadn't explained anything to him. He had no way of knowing why she was upset. Still. He should have told her he had a son.

She should have told him she didn't want kids.

Kat was determined to get through her day without any more thoughts of Gerard. She responded to her mom's text about going out to dinner that night. Her mom seemed more than happy to go out, and she promised to pay too, which wasn't like her. Kat turned her phone off again as soon as she had confirmed their dinner reservations.

Her plan to get involved in work and ignore her life was scuttled when a huge bouquet of dark blue hyacinths arrived for her late in the afternoon. She didn't need to read the card to know they were from Gerard.

She held the closed envelope for a long time before she opened the card. She had fallen hard for a guy with a kid. She honestly didn't know how to approach her own desire to not have any. Even if she might be able to come to grips with the fact he already had one.

"I don't know what I did wrong. Please answer my texts. In AGONY. G."

She ran over the scene from the morning. He had been laying on his back talking freely. He was clearly not trying to hide anything from her. He was completely surprised by her abrupt departure.

And she hadn't told him about her complete and total ban on children in her life. It was hard enough to tell a man she wasn't going to have sex with him, let alone that she never, ever, would have his children. Finding out that he had one meant that, if they developed their relationship at all, she would have some relationship with that child.

What would it be like to be a step-mother? The question popped into her head. Maybe a lot like being an aunt? She'd watched Margaret's two-year-old daughter over a weekend just before the second baby came. It had been fun. She knew going into it was a forty-eight-hour stint and would be over at a specified time. Wouldn't having a step-son be like that with weekend visits?

Fifteen minutes later, another bouquet arrived, this one was white and red roses. The card said, "Your silence is deafening."

Her stomach flipped and twisted. She wanted to call him. Tell him she'd been an idiot, but what could she really say when she had no idea what she really wanted other than him. Oh, she knew that she wanted him beyond a doubt.

She arranged the two bouquets on her desk. She did a quick search to see what the internet had to say about the colors of flowers. Hyacinths, apparently, were the official flowers for general apologies. She'd always thought red roses were for love, white for weddings. The blend was an apology to someone you love.

Is this what Gerard really meant? Did he love her? He was a scientist and brilliant, but were the flowers a deeper message to her or was she reading them wrong, or was she crazy to even try to give them more meaning then they had? Did he have any idea what he was apologizing for?

The hyacinths' sweet scent filled her office, even overcoming the lack-luster scent of the roses. While picture perfect, the roses had none of the rich sweetness a good rose should have.

She re-read all his text messages. His obvious confused pleas for her to call him ate at her conscious. He deserved a response from her. She sent him a text, hoping that it would clarify things.

K: *You have a child. I need time to think.*

She waited. Less than five seconds later he texted back.

G: *We need to talk in person. Tonight.*

K: *I have plans with my Mom tonight.*

G: *I don't like long silences. I'll wait for you Katherine, but not for ever...*

Chapter 27

Her mother downed her scotch and gasped with the sting of it. She wiped her lips with her napkin before speaking. "You know, Katherine, you're being a complete idiot over this."

Katherine looked at her mom in complete disbelief. She hadn't expected her mom to take his side, but she'd hoped for a little more compassion than this. She used to just internalize her feelings, but now, she didn't have room to stuff any more feelings inside. Katherine put her own glass down on the table, harder than she expected to.

"Did you ever stop to think about me? About what kind of affect your having kids would have on me? My whole childhood wasn't about having fun at the park, it was about taking care of everyone else."

"I know you've always wanted something different

from life than I had. I get that you didn't want to be pregnant and married at 18, mother of ten kids. But, it was my choice to make."

Katherine was pretty sure it wasn't just her mother's choice. "Dad wanted more kids than ten, though, didn't he?"

Her mother waved at the waitress and pointed at her glass, silently ordering another round for both of them.

"As I told you, my choice was to have ten children. I was done after that."

"Your body was done. I heard that fight between you and Dad, the one where you admitted to having your tubes tied behind his back."

Her mother shrugged. "Like I said. My choices. But, what I want you to know is I'm happy."

"With what choice? Are you happy about being here waiting for Dad to notice you're gone?"

"We've had our ups and downs, your father and I, but I have no doubt that we will be back where we need to be soon enough."

"When is that going to be mom?"

"I'm sorry to be such a burden on you with my presence."

Katherine closed her eyes and sucked in a few deep breaths of air. "Can we make this about me for a while? I'm in love with someone who has a kid. I don't want kids."

"I am sorry about that. I didn't realize until you were older just what a strain all your brothers and sisters had on you, personally. I thought you liked helping out."

"A strain? You think that's all that it was? I diapered them. I fed them. I took care of them. You know, they all call me before they call you. I help them figure out what to tell you so you don't freak out."

"But, they're your siblings, not your children. That's what siblings do. They get help from and support each other."

They felt like they were hers. Should she just let it go? Start living her own life? Let her brothers and sisters go?

Her mom leaned forward and patted Katherine's hand. "Why not relax into this new kind of relationship and then see where you want to go? Get used to actually having sex with a man. Get over that irrational fear of yours about getting pregnant. It might not work out."

The condescending tone was too much for Katherine. "How could you say that to me? I haven't had sex in fifteen years because of the way I grew up. It's not like I'm trying out a new vacuum."

"You need to consider that throwing away Gerard

just because he has a child in his life, is throwing away the baby with the bath-water, literally. He might be the perfect man for you. Why would you want to give that up?"

"I don't want children. It's like you don't get me at all."

First, Carleen had called her neurotic. Now her mother was calling her irrational. Was she totally off base on this? Plenty of people didn't want kids. There was nothing wrong with her, but her mom still didn't understand. Would she ever? Would her mom ever see how much her choices had impacted Kat?

Her connection with Gerard was a profound and deep one. Should she give that up just because he had a child with someone else?

Do you believe in love at first sight?

"Mom, if I continue on this path, I don't think there's any way out of it. I'm in love. I've never been in love. Not like this."

"You're re-writing history. What about Willie Simpson when you were a junior in high school? I seem to recall some love-talk back then. And then there was Bucky."

"I was crushing on him. That's all." But Katherine wondered if there was some truth to what her mother had been saying. This thing with Gerard was different. *Really different.*

"Raising a step-son, especially if his mom is involved, is not going to be anything remotely like having your own kid. You can set your terms. You don't have to be the mom. You can be the step-mom. And, frankly, you're totally going about this the wrong way."

"Going about this the wrong way? Thanks Mom. I need some time. Besides, your relationship isn't exactly something I want to emulate."

Her mother downed the drink the waiter had put in front of her. "I never said your life had to be anything like mine, Kat. But my life works well for me. I am sorry it impacted you so negatively, but you really did turn out okay, sweetie."

"Great, Mom. Thanks. It doesn't look like it's working all that wonderful for you right now."

"It's just the way I want it to be. We all have our ways of being Kat, and you have made it abundantly clear you're not thrilled with mine."

"I just don't get it. All these years with you and Dad doing this escape and retrieval game. What do you get out of it?"

"Every time your father shows up to get me, it reinforces how much he loves me. And, I know he does, Katherine. He has always been clear about that in spite of all his messes."

"Didn't you ever think of the example you were

setting for all of us? How it would affect us? The cost it had on us?"

Her mother put down her drink and reached out both hands to Katherine. "I had no idea you had these rules about your boyfriends. I just figured you hadn't found Mr. Right yet. And, I certainly don't see you as someone who hates children."

Kat frowned. "I have never hated children. I love them. Other people's children. Your children...I adore all of them."

"As an oldest sister should. I'm sorry you ever felt like you were more to them than that. It was probably short-sighted of me, but honestly, what can I do about it now? You're thirty years old, Kat. So, I think you need to move on from here. Blame me all you want, but I can't go back and change the past, no matter how much I wish I could."

Kat didn't need her to go change the past. But, it was sweet to hear what was sure to be the closest to an apology her mother would ever come to giving her.

The food arrived and they ate in an oddly companionable silence.

"I should probably at least talk to him," Katherine admitted.

A familiar voice boomed from behind her. "Talk to who?"

Katherine sprang up. "Daddy?"

"Heya pumpkin." He lifted her in a bear hug off her feet and swung her in a full circle before setting her back down again. Once she was settled, he stood next to the table. "Mary. Time to come home."

The triumphant knowing look in her mother's eyes startled Katherine. It wasn't a surprise, this is pretty much the exact same thing that always happened. It was a relief, though. She would be leaving her apartment, probably tonight. Her sister had sounded so certain they were heading for divorce.

"Well, it took you long enough. Did you finally get tired of that old sourpuss?"

"Do you really want the details?" He pulled out one of the extra chairs at the table and sat down. The waitress appeared out of nowhere with a new scotch for her mom and a menu for her dad. He waved it away and ordered an IPA.

"Hey, Dad, how did you find us here?"

He pulled out his phone. "I have your mom on an app. And she has me on hers, don't you darling?"

She lifted an eyebrow in agreement, though she was looking a little peeved that he had found them.

"I texted your mother before I got on the plane, but she didn't respond."

"That's why you were so intent on going out to dinner? You didn't want to be at my apartment? So Daddy couldn't find you?"

"Well, I forgot about that damn app, or I would have turned it off to make it harder for him to find us."

"Dad, you knew about the GPS thing Mom put on your phone?"

He grinned. "Why do you think I left it over at Lois' house for a couple of days? I figured it would get her going a little bit. Plus, two days without my phone was pretty sweet."

"I talked to Joan. She told me you were home, so I knew you weren't actually over there this whole time." She grabbed his hands between hers.

"Sweetie. I'm sorry. You know I will always love you," he said.

They kissed.

Katherine loved her parents, and she was sure they loved each other, but they were messed up in too many ways to count. "I think me leaving is a good idea. I'll see you back at my place."

As she got up to leave, her father grabbed her by the hand and pulled it close to his heart. "Love you, baby girl. See you in a bit."

It was then that something entirely new clicked for her. Her father was oblivious. He'd come home at the end of most days, had his dinner and did something with a child. He was active in their lives, but not all at once. And the thing that really hit home was that she had a huge capacity to love people.

She loved her siblings even though she resented caring for them. She loved her parents even though she resented their weird arrangement that made it necessary for her to do so much of the child care. And yet, she had no doubt that her parents loved her. She left them at the restaurant and slowly walked back to her apartment. The cherry blossoms were in full bloom, and the walk along the river was calming.

The entire walk back, all she could think about was Gerard and how little she knew about him. How she really didn't have any idea what was going on with him and his son. She had to find out, she had to know if her feelings about him were true...

Chapter 28

Tomorrow. So much had already happened, that all Kat wanted to do was relax. She was exhausted. At home, she changed into her most comfortable pair of sweats and an old Capitals jersey. She'd dated one of their goalies for a while, and she always felt sort of buff while wearing it, like some of his gruffness on the ice managed to rub off onto her and toughen her up a bit.

He'd lasted maybe six months at arms lengths, but had dumped her when he wanted more than she was willing to give him. He was married and had a kid within a year.

Her mother had picked up the apartment more in the last four days than it had been in months, so there wasn't any monotonous tasks for Katherine to do. She went through the mail. Texted Margaret and Michael about Dad's arrival, asked them to pass the message on to everyone else.

She heard her parent's voices approach her door and dropped down onto the sofa, faking a nonchalant position that wouldn't fool anyone, especially her parents. She stuck with it anyway, quickly grabbing a magazine to pretend to read.

"Hey, that didn't take too long," she said.

Her mother pointed to Dad, and then the armchair across from Katherine. "You sit there while I go grab my things."

Her father settled in across from her. "What's troubling you, Katherine?"

"Me? What makes you think I'm troubled?"

He pointed at the magazine. "As far as I know, you still usually read things right side up, don't you?"

She was holding the magazine upside down. "Oh. Right." She tossed it onto the coffee table. "Mom already told you, didn't she?"

"About your young man problem? She gave me the basic sketch. And, I'm sorry you had to find out about *our* little arrangement like that. It's pretty personal and certainly won't work for everyone, but we thought everyone in the family knew about it."

"Mom swears she's good with it most of the time."

"Yeah, well I slip up occasionally. But, I am getting

older, and I need to pay more attention to how I go about things."

Katherine held up her hands. "Don't give me any details. I do not want the details."

"Fine. Fine. Pumpkin. I just want you to know that we love you and know you will do whatever is right for you."

"Thanks Daddy. I appreciate that."

"But, you'd be a fool to pass up real love if that's what you've found with this Gerard fellow."

"I never saw myself raising kids."

"Love is precious, Kitty-Kat. You need to hold onto it when you find it. Children just make that love better."

A few more minutes and her parents would be gone. She hadn't even considered asking her dad to stay a couple of days for a visit. She just wanted to be alone so she could lick her wounds and figure out things on her own. She was hating the fact she'd have to wait until the next day to clear things up with Gerard.

"Your mother told me about how you feel about all the work you did growing up." He put his hands on her shoulders. "I'm really sorry about that. I never really thought much about it because I saw you alone so often. I was gone a lot."

Katherine reigned in the residual anger. He was

trying. Besides, what good would rehashing it all do for her? "Thank you, Daddy. It helps just for you to acknowledge it."

She felt a little better already. Having her parents both acknowledge her contribution to the family was something she'd never known she'd needed so badly.

The door buzzer made her jump. She opened the door to find Gerard holding a gigantic bunch of red roses up to her with a look of complete bewilderment on his face.

"I don't know what I did, but you running out this morning was the scariest thing that has ever happened to me. I couldn't wait until tomorrow."

Her father stepped up behind her, making his presence more obvious.

Katherine closed her eyes wishing her parents would disappear. "Daddy, meet Gerard. Gerard, this is Malcolm O'Malley, my father."

Gerard reached out a hand, and her father grasped it tightly, man to man, as if he were appraising Gerard.

Her mother appeared just then with her suitcase. "I'm ready to go."

"You must have been packed already," Katherine said.

"Of course I was. Your father texted me from the airport, remember?"

Her father kissed her on the cheek as he pointedly

led her mother away from Gerard and out to the car. "Give us a call tomorrow. We can meet for lunch before we go back to Chicago."

She watched them go, Gerard had come inside and was now at her side. Once they were alone, Gerard turned to face her. His eyes were serious.

"Talk."

Chapter 29

"You have a kid."

He handed her the roses, and she buried her face in them. They were rich and sweet, just the way roses should be.

"And what is it to you? We just met. I don't go around telling people everything about me just when I meet them."

"We slept together. We had sex. When were you going to tell me?"

"You left the hotel this morning when you overheard me talking to Jake and his mom."

"Yeah."

"Why didn't you just stay and talk to me this morning? For someone who is so open and honest about sex stuff, I'm disappointed in the rest of your communication skills."

Katherine hadn't expected that. She was an excellent communicator. Wasn't she?

"I had a right to know."

"Because we had sex? Once?"

Their encounter *was* just another fling to him. She backed away from him until her calves hit the sofa and she curled onto it, pulling her knees up to her chest.

"I thought what we had was special." She *had* built it up more than it was for him. For her, this whole thing had been huge. For him, it had been another conquest. "I thought what we had was unique."

"Katherine, what we have *is* unique, and it *is* special. But it's new. There's a lot about me you don't know. I would have told you about Jake, if you would have let me." He ran his hands through his hair. "Honestly, we just never got a chance to talk about it. I don't usually bring him up unless I've been seeing someone a few times."

Katherine turned her head away from him.

"Katherine, the fact I have a child is just one thing about me you don't know. There are thousands of things you don't know about me. Are you going to freak out every time I reveal something about me you don't like?"

He sat next to her so that she was facing him.

"Is my having a child a deal breaker for you? Just the fact I *have* him?"

She felt low. Ridiculous. The way he put it made her come across as insipid and self-centered.

"Get to know me, really know who I am before you decide whether or not you can handle a relationship with me and my son."

"It just seemed like such a basic thing. We did talk a lot the other night, and you didn't bring him up. It's kind of a natural thing to bring up your kids. I told you about my parents. My brothers and sisters? We talked for hours. Both nights. In all of that time you didn't say a single word."

Gerard held up his hands. "Okay, fine. Let me tell you more about myself. First, I have one child. A son who is going into kindergarten next year. He lives with his mother, someone I admire greatly, but to whom I have never been married."

His voice was harsh. Katherine wasn't entirely sure if he was being facetious or serious.

"I hate rice in any way shape or form. As a consequence, I am one of five people on the planet who hates sushi. I will not, ever, eat sushi. Is that a problem for you?"

He was on a roll now. "Oh, and I don't like jazz. Even fun jazz. I'm a rock and roll kinda guy, and I like music I can sing to because I like singing aloud while I do the dishes. I also know almost all the lyrics to every

Rogers and Hammerstein musical. I like singing them when I do housework. Is that going to drive you bonkers?"

Katherine held up her hands in supplication. He had made his point, and she felt the rush of embarrassment color her cheeks. He grasped her face in his hands.

"Katherine, I don't know you either. I know you have nine siblings. I'm getting that you are wigged out about Jake. I know you have slightly crazy parents. I know you work for Lincoln Pierce and might end up in some highly political spotlights. I know you have a gay best friend. More importantly, I know there's a connection between us I can't explain. I'm hoping that you might just love me enough to explore being with me before dropping me just because I have a child."

"I don't know how I feel," she said, hating the false tone in her voice. She knew damned well how she felt. "I don't believe in love at first sight." It was a weak excuse, she knew it.

He knew it.

"I didn't either, Katherine. Right up until Friday night."

Do you believe in love at first sight?

He kissed her, and she didn't fight when he pulled her into his arms. Maybe she was being unreasonable.

One child in her life wasn't anything like nine. Kindergarten meant there wouldn't be any diapers. He would still have his mother to worry about him. She still wasn't sure.

"Gerard, I just don't know. I'm afraid that if I go all in with you…"

"You'll end up having to be part of Jake's life."

"Yeah."

She loved her sister Margaret's children, didn't she?

"Get to know me for who I am before you try to make up your mind. Then we can talk about Jake, okay?"

Maybe she could handle being a step-mom. It might not be too terribly horrible. She knew, deep down, her mother was wrong about one thing—her love for Gerard was real and not going to disappear.

But he was focusing in on Jake as the problem here. She needed to tell him she wasn't going to have children. She could be setting herself up for a really bad heartbreak if she didn't tell him the whole truth now.

She turned away from him to screw up her courage. She wasn't sure she could say what she needed to if she was looking at him. "This thing isn't just about Jake. It's about kids." This could be the deal-breaker. Better to let him leave now, before they became more attached to each other.

He placed his hands on her shoulders and squeezed. "Come on Katherine. We can't have any secrets between us if we want this to work."

She took strength from him. "I don't want to have children. It's not some weird fear of bearing them. It's the kids themselves. I don't want to deal with all that again." She turned back to face him.

His face was screwed up in confusion. "Again? What do you mean, again?"

"Weren't you listening the other night when I bared my soul about all my siblings?"

"I was, but I didn't think you were complaining about them. You sounded like someone who loved them, not resented them."

"I don't resent them. I resent my mother for making me take care of them."

There. She had said it. And for some reason, just saying it out loud to someone who cared about her made all the difference. Gerard stepped back and examined her head to toe. She felt more exposed now than she had when she was standing in front of him completely naked.

"Okay. I have to admit. I'm not sure what to do with this information."

"I'm afraid of falling in love with you and you walking out on me when you figure out you're not going to change my mind about having children."

"You're telling me this now to pre-empt me from falling in love with you? If I want more kids I should leave now?"

"Yes. I just want to be clear. Getting into a relationship with me, means we will never have children. If it gets serious, I'll ask you to make that permanent."

He shook his head. "Wow."

"Gerard?"

He held up his hands in a helpless gesture. "I don't know what to say Katherine. I don't know that I can make that commitment right this second."

He backed away from her and opened the door. "I think I need some time."

"Gerard?"

"What, Katherine? Did you think you could lay a bomb like that on me and expect me to just say, 'Hey, I've got one kid, I'm good.' Jake was...an accident. I wasn't even in love with his mom. And I love him more than...anything. I want that again. I *thought* I wanted that again, but while really being in love with the mother. Being a partner in parenting. The whole love, marriage, and baby carriage. You talked about your family with such love, I assumed you wanted that, too."

"I don't know what to tell you. I don't want kids." She was unable to move. She wasn't sure what she wanted anymore. She wasn't sure what she felt—

except for an overwhelming need to be with Gerard, but she didn't know how to tell him.

Gerard's body slumped and his expression was so sad. He simply turned around and walked out. Kat watched the door slam shut behind him.

She'd fucked it up completely.

Chapter 30

Kat unfroze herself and ran to the door to chase after Gerard. But, he was nowhere to be seen. She should have moved faster. She turned off the lights and made her way to her bedroom. It was suddenly very lonely in her apartment. She climbed onto her bed without bothering to change, and pulled in a pillow. The tears came easily to her. She went over every word she'd had with Gerard.

She had told him several stories about her brothers and sisters. She could kind of see how she might have come across as having been proud of them. How she loved them.

She tried to sleep, but her mind churned and whirred through the night and into the dawn. Her alarm went off at its usual time. She sat up and mechanically dressed for her run with Kenny.

He would help her think through this.

She walked, rather than ran, to their meeting point and he was there doing some extra stretches. "You are so late. Come on girl, get moving."

He paused in his hamstring stretch as she neared, his eyes bulging out at her appearance.

"Oh no. What happened? You look like you spent the night in a dumpster that got set on fire."

She told him everything about her parents and then Gerard. "Maybe I shouldn't have said anything. I would have gotten a few months of happiness out of all this."

Kenny shook his head. "Kitty-Kat you are missing the point. You were absolutely right in telling the man you think you are in love with your truth. But your truth is what is so fucked up."

Kat tilted her head back over hunched shoulders. "Oh, not you, too."

"Yeah, me too. You keep saying you don't want to have kids. But I don't think that's what you really mean. You keep telling yourself that, and you keep telling others that, but you've got it wrong."

"I've got it wrong? Really? How is that possible, Kenny?"

"I'm not one to say you should have kids. I'll never have kids. I know this. But as your friend, I know you. I get that you love kids, but you don't want nine kids. All

I'm saying is keep an open mind, don't say absolutely no."

Kat slumped to the ground next to Kenny. He did a side stretch. "Think about it. You don't want to pass it on. What's really going on here isn't what about what happened to you so much as what you're afraid of doing to them."

"Them?"

"Your own kids. You're afraid you'll fuck them up."

Kat blinked several times as she took in what he had said. "Maybe. I guess you could be right."

"Can you tell me how many things you and Gerard have in common with your parents?"

Kat shook her head. "Uhm...not many."

"See. You're already off to a better start than they were."

"My dad is an attorney. He makes pretty good money."

"But not as much as Gerard and you are going to be pulling in. You work full time, your mother did not. Gerard is working private sector for profit, right? A lobbyist? His net worth is already at over two million bucks."

Kat looked at him sideways. "I told you to drop the background check."

"Hah. He was never married to Jakes' mom, but they made an agreement that she would go back to school as soon as Gerard was settled into his career and Jake was in kindergarten. That's about to happen. But you can afford a nanny. You can afford house-cleaners. You can afford to be as aloof as you want."

"I don't want to be aloof. "

"Ha! See? I was right."

Kat could see his point, but it wasn't as simple as all that. She wasn't convinced she wanted to have children so much as she was no longer so sure that she was absolutely dead set against them. She didn't want to inflict her childhood on anyone else. She'd learned a couple of important things over the last few days, the least of which is she needed to work on communications...and that included with herself.

She copied Kenny's stretch and put her head on her outstretched knee. She was so tired, she might take the day off work. Her parents would be leaving in the afternoon, so she could use their presence as an excuse. There was a lull in her duties for a couple of days before things would heat back up again.

"Maybe I should fly back to Chicago with my parents."

"Why would you do that? Kat, you'd be running away."

She slapped the side of her head. "I'd be just like my mom. God, Kenny, I am so much like my mom, aren't I?"

"It hurts to realize, doesn't it?"

"I ruined everything with Gerard."

"Offer him a compromise."

"What do you suggest?"

"Start with you not wanting him to get snipped tomorrow for one. That is a definite turn off for most men."

"Okay. I think I can manage that one. What else do you suggest oh, munificent one?"

"You might consider telling him you'd reconsider the whole kid thing in a year or two."

She switched to her other leg. "I don't know. I'm not liking that one."

"Love and marriage is about compromise. If you want that big wedding with the dream man waiting for you at the end of the aisle, you need to be open to some options, honey."

Kate was worried she'd compromise her whole self out of things if she wasn't too careful.

"But, if you need Gerard in your life, you might find it worth it."

Kenny jumped up and pulled her to her feet. "We need to get a move on it. We're running double time now."

Chapter 31

Katherine felt loads better by the time she jogged into the driveway of her apartment complex. Kenny was right. Compromise in relationships was important. She could compromise herself totally into being a step-mom. She'd worked that part out even before Gerard had showed up at her door the previous night.

Compromising herself into actually having a kid? She wasn't sure about that yet, but maybe she didn't have to make that kind of promise right now. She'd call Gerard. Apologize. Try to work things out.

She rounded the corner toward her building. Gerard sat on the stoop with his back against the door. He was looking pretty disheveled and wearing the same clothes he had the night before.

She slowed to a walk when she saw him, worried

that she'd mess things up further if she rushed up to him. Talking with Kenny had helped a lot, but she thought she'd have a little more time to get her act together.

She stopped a few feet away from him.

Gerard ran a hand through his hair and looked up at her with blood-shot red-rimmed eyes. "I couldn't leave things the way they were. I...I honestly never really thought about more kids before yesterday. Other than a general desire to have a family. Kat, I have Jake, and he's not going away, but I'm not tied to any one particular image for my future."

He stood up. "I've spent the last few hours thinking about things. If you feel so strongly about not having kids...well...I can see that. I am willing to go into this thing fully, both feet first knowing that you might never change your mind about that. But, can we not do anything permanent for...I don't know...five years?"

"Five years?" Her heart ached with desire to reach out and touch him, to run her fingers through the rough mop of hair. He saw them being together at least that long? "And what if we don't agree at the end of five years?"

"I can agree to that."

She knew in five years, she would be in so deep she'd never let him go. "You know I have nine siblings.

I'm already an aunt four times over. There will always be children in our life."

He wrapped his arms around her. "I love you Katherine. No matter what happens, we can make this work."

They leaned into her door as they kissed each other, holding each other tight. They stumbled into her living room, and fell onto the couch together. Her tears made his face all blurry, but she didn't care. She knew she was going to be late for work, but she didn't care. All she cared about was her and Gerard in this room. Light seemed to fill it up, where it had been so dark yesterday.

He found the roses he'd brought last night, tore off the petals and tossed them around her. The aromatic smell filled the room. Then, he bent down onto the couch and pulled her up so she stood next to him.

"I believe in love at first sight."

He pressed his forehead against hers. She suddenly knew she'd be able to follow his lead. This would be a Tango for a lifetime.

More by Juno Chase

The DC Knights series can be read in any order, but we hope you don't miss any of them!

New to the Game—D.C. Knights Book 1

Chloe's the new intern, but she jumps into the game both feet first.

Playing For Keeps—D.C. Knights Book 2

Katherine thinks she's got things figured out until a sexy scientist tangos his way into her heart.

All In—D.C. Knights Book 3

Madeline has no problem playing games until she meets Ewan a man who knows how to treat her like a woman.

Fair and Square—D.C. Knights Book 4

Lizbeth doesn't have time for games, but she ends up in the midst of a political game no one in Congressman Pierce's office saw coming.

Only Bluffing—D.C. Knights Book 5

Eleanor Winslow and Daniel Prado are from different worlds. Will their love overcome dark histories and ancient legacies?

Game On—D.C. Knights Book 6

Cheyenne LeFleur lives on the wild side. Will Alexander Moore be able to handle her history, or will he reject her like so many before him?

For the Win—D.C. Knights Book 7 The final chapter in this series. Congressman Lincoln Pierce deserves love, too. Can he find it while maintaining his principles?

Also by Juno Chase:

ARTIFACT of BETRAYAL: an exciting romantic suspense novel

If you had to choose between saving your life or the love of your life, *who would you choose?*

Claire Townsend has it all, a great job, her own shop in Brooklyn, until one night when she loses everything. With thirteen days to pay off a dangerous loan shark, she decides to partake in a black-market smuggling operation to save her own neck.

Bruno Canul is an archeologist who works as a consultant with the FBI. He chases a suspect to Belize only to find the ex-love-of-his-life as part of the crew. He can't tell if he should trust Claire or if she's joined forces with the smuggler.

Afraid her choices will get Bruno killed, Claire tries to resist falling back in love with him. If she goes through with the smuggling scheme, she can pay off her loan, but she'd lose Bruno's love and trust *forever*. If she stands up for their love, she's a dead woman.

This adventurous romantic suspense is sure to keep you on the edge of your seat as Claire and Bruno find love in the jungle and ancient Mayan ruins of Belize.

About Juno Chase

Who said chivalry is dead? They were totally wrong! We love, love, love hot guys who are modern day knights and heroes but also know how to heat things up between the sheets.

Juno Chase is the nom de plume of two married moms who love reading and writing happy stories. We wanted to see these modern day knights celebrated in romance, so here we are. We're not a big group of people writing—there is just the two of us. We both spend lots of time reading and writing in each story to bring you the most complete, hot, and exciting stories possible.

Thank you so much for reading *New to the Game*, we hope you enjoyed reading it as much as we did writing it. If you sign up for our newsletter, you will be the first to know whenever we have a new book available.

Follow Juno Chase on your favorite social Media. We'd love to hear from you!

www.Junochase.com
juno@junochase.com

Acknowledgments

We'd like to thank a few people who helped us get this book into your lovely hands, dear readers. We are part of an amazing writing group who has listened to our ideas, helped us with plotting, and given us some straight feedback. We couldn't have done this without your energy and help-—you ladies rock! Thank you for all your reading time and thoughtful suggestions to help make the D.C. Knights series a reality.

To our intrepid beta readers. Thank you for taking the time to read and give us honest criticism. Especially to Dawn who has faithfully read everything we've handed her and keeps asking for more! Funny enough, we need to thank another Dawn for her awesome editing and catching all those typos—we hope!

And to our families—our fabulous husbands and children who have supported us in so many different ways and picked up the pieces as needed. We love you!

www.ingramcontent.com/pod-product-compliance
Lightning Source LLC
Chambersburg PA
CBHW032121180726